Terrible Tales:

The Absolutely, Positively, 100 Percent TRUE Stories of Cinderella, Little Red Riding Hood, Those Three Greedy Pigs, Hairy Rapunzel, and the Utterly Horrible Brats, Hansel and Gretel as Told at the Beginning of Time

Terrible Tales:

The Absolutely, Positively, 100 Percent TRUE Stories of Cinderella, Little Red Riding Hood, Those Three Greedy Pigs, Hairy Rapunzel, and the Utterly Horrible Brats, Hansel and Gretel as Told at the Beginning of Time

As presented by Felicitatus Miserius

With a Foreword and Backword by Sir Jasper Gowlings
And Illustrations by Shirley Chiang

iUniverse, Inc.
New York   Bloomington

Terrible Tales

The Absolutely, Positively, 100 Percent TRUE Stories of
Cinderella, Little Red Riding Hood, Those Three Greedy
Pigs, Hairy Rapunzel, and the Utterly Horrible Brats,
Hansel and Gretel as Told at the Beginning of Time

iUniverse books may be ordered through booksellers or by contacting:

iUniverse
1663 Liberty Drive
Bloomington, IN 47403
www.iuniverse.com
1-800-Authors (1-800-288-4677)

Because of the dynamic nature of the Internet, any Web addresses or links
contained in this book may have changed since publication and may no longer be
valid. The views expressed in this work are solely those of the author and do not
necessarily reflect the views of the publisher, and the publisher hereby disclaims
any responsibility for them.

ISBN: 978-1-4401-4209-3 (sc)
ISBN: 978-1-4401-4211-6 (dj)
ISBN: 978-1-4401-4210-9 (ebook)

Library of Congress Control Number: 2009927677

Printed in the United States of America

iUniverse rev. date: 8/25/2009

This book is dedicated to all children who have ever been bullied and who have ever wished that they were taller, shorter, thinner, fatter, better-looking, wealthier, more talented, more popular, more anything. Please know that you are perfect just the way you are. Don't ever let anyone make you believe otherwise.

My heartfelt wish for you, from now until the end of forever, is that you live happily ever after.

And, I must tell you, my wishes always come true.

Contents

Foreword

One day, not so long ago, I was startled to hear a knock
at my front door.
As you can well imagine, I fainted dead away.
When I awoke three weeks later, the knock came again.
I fainted for a second time.

And, dear friend, that might have been the end of this
story—for surely I would have died of starvation or of a burst
bladder—if the door hadn't suddenly been blown off its hinges
by a strange and powerful gust of wind. Dust and leaves and dead
flies swirled through my front room, making it impossible to see
and extraordinarily difficult to breathe.

When the debris storm finally started to subside, I could
make out a person standing on my front step. But what an odd
person—or thing—it was.

It was wrapped from head to toe in a moldy, moth-eaten cape
that smelt strongly of wet dog and split pea soup ... a combina-
tion of scents that made me feel strangely hungry. It appeared to
be about the size of a two year old, but its wrinkled, wizened face
suggested a person at least five hundred times that age.

In the presence of such a bizarre individual, I found myself
prepared to faint for a third time, but was stopped in my tracks
by a screech that was emitted from the depths of the cape. "Don't
even think about it, you sniveling, miserable son of a cur," the
creature's voice scratched and scritched.

Egads! The thing was clearly a fiend straight from the depths of hell! Son of a cur indeed! I suddenly felt far too annoyed to faint. Instead, I shot back rather smartly, if I do say so myself, "What do you want, you mangy old mutt? And how dare you darken my doorstop … not to mention blow the door clean off its hinges … for I'm sure that was your doing, you puny, pungent parasite. I'll expect you to pay for the damages, you can be sure of that."

The creature cackled rudely; and then, before I had time to give it a swift boot in the backside to send it on its way, a deformed claw shot out from the cape and the thing grasped my wrist. Heavens above! It was going to steal my solid gold watch!

But no … instead of ripping my precious timepiece from my person, it pulled out a gilt-edged, leather-bound book from beneath the stinky folds of its costume. This it thrust at me with an aggressive grunt and a vulgar noise that sounded suspiciously like a belch.

When I did nothing but stand there dumbfounded, disgusted by the horrific noises it was producing, it kicked me in the stomach and then pushed the book at me again, grunting and burping menacingly.

Being an intelligent, intuitive person, I assumed it wanted me to take the smelly old volume from its hideous claw. So, wishing to avoid further physical injury, I reached out and took the book from it with my one free hand.

No sooner had I done this then the creature kicked me in the stomach once more—"for good luck," it said (although whether it meant good luck for it or for me was not clear)—and then vanished in another swirling gust of fly corpses and dust mites.

I took the book with me to the kitchen where I studied it carefully while eating a chunk of green, hairy cheese on a slice of moldy bread. (It would seem that my three weeks of unconsciousness had reduced the contents of my ice box to piles of rotting, putrid, unrecognizable bits of mildew and fluff. Ah well.

There are worse things to eat than mold and mildew, I can assure you.)

On close inspection of the ancient, rotting book, I found that it contained stories that closely resembled the fairy tales I had read and believed as a young and innocent child. The tales in this ancient manuscript, however, all ended quite dreadfully, in a manner that curdled my blood and made my hair stand on end with horror.

I would have burned the cursed book if it had not been for a letter that I found thrust between its crumbling pages. Written in a spidery scrawl, the letter read as follows:

To All Those Who Find Themselves in Possession of These Magical and Portentous Tales…

Know that you are hereby bound by elfin law to share the teachings found herein with the rest of the world and to set right the dangerous and erroneous impressions left by later, distorted versions of the truth.

The tales which you are about to read are the veritable, unembellished accounts of events that took place soon after the dawn of time. Learn from these stories and you will find your heart's desire … BUT— and harken to this warning most carefully—ignore the lessons they teach and doom and despair will be your lot forever.

The choice is yours in this and in all things. Choose wisely and well.

Yours in pain or in pleasure,
Felicitatus Miserius
May 23, 1244 AD

Oh, how I shudder each time I read those spine-tingling words!

And, oh, how deeply I regret having to share them and their terrible threats with you … because, of course, you are now bound by elfin law just as I am. But, dear reader, you must see that, as much as I did truly wish to spare you any pain, discomfort, and eternal anguish, I had no alternative but to force you into this wretched situation in order to escape certain death myself.

You will find in the pages of this publication a faithful recounting of the cursed book's contents in their appalling entirety.

Heed the letter's warning and study the tales well, I beg of you.

Oh, yes … and by the way … the ancient crone, who I now understand was none other than Felicitatus Miserius herself, did indeed steal my solid gold watch.

Take pains to protect your possessions if she should appear at *your* door one miserable day. For she just might … and most likely will.

Your friend,
Sir Jasper Gowlings

Cinderella

Once upon a time, when goblins and witches and fairy godmothers still roamed the earth openly, there lived a beautiful girl named Cinderella. As many accounts of Cinderella's life would have it, this young girl was as lovely and kind and good as she was pretty.

This, I'm sad to say, is a colossal, shamefaced lie.

Cinderella was, in fact, one of the meanest, wickedest girls who ever walked the face of the earth. She loved nothing better than to torment the people and other living creatures that were unfortunate enough to cross her path.

Now, you would think that this shouldn't and wouldn't be the case, seeing as Cinderella was lucky enough to live in a magnificent, big stone house, surrounded by gorgeous flowering gardens, a lush, green forest, and acres and acres of fertile fields in one of the finest parts of merry olde England. She had servants to tend to her every desire, beautiful dresses to wear, and a mother and father who adored her.

But, it would seem that all of this good fortune, wealth, and love only made Cinderella the wickeder. She believed, you see, that all of her advantages in life gave her the right to treat other people however she wanted. And she wanted to treat them badly. Very badly indeed.

One of her favorite pastimes was to trot down to the kitchen whenever her parents hosted a lavish dinner party. She would wait until Cook had turned her back, and then she would hastily drop worms, beetles, and other savory insects into the luscious soups, stews, and pies that Cook was preparing, where they would remain safely nestled until the dinner guests started chewing on them. Oh, how happy it made her to watch the guests faint when they bit off the head of a cockroach thinking it was a carrot, or throw up bucketfuls of soup when they chomped on a worm, which they had mistaken for a noodle. And she would literally stand on her head with glee when the poor cook was thrown into prison for trying to poison them all.

But, as much as she enjoyed slipping creepy crawlies into other people's food, there was nothing that brought Cinderella quite so much pleasure as rolling about in the soot and the cinders that lined the grates of the many fireplaces that heated the rooms of her huge country house. In fact, it was because she took such delight in this activity, that her father had blessed her with the loving nickname of "Cinder-ella". He thought her taste for collecting dirt was quite charming when she first began exhibiting this fine behavior as a toddler. The laundresses didn't consider the habit quite so charming, however, as the filthy state of Cinderella's clothes created a great deal of extra work and heartache for them. Cinderella would change out of one outfit and into another as soon as she had gotten the first one nicely blackened (which usually took about fifteen minutes), and then she would run down to the dark, steamy laundry room with it. There she would find the laundresses toiling over huge vats of soapy, boiling water, with mountains of Cinderella's clothes piled around them. She would hurl her sooty garment at them and yell, "Hurry up, you lazy loiterers. If you don't get these dresses cleaned, I'll soon have nothing to wear." She would then kick them in their backsides to try to help them along and would charge back upstairs to find another fireplace to roll about in. Many a laundress had suffered a complete nervous collapse trying to keep up with the thousands of dresses that had to be washed, scrubbed, de-sooted and de-cindered every day and, every once in a while, one of them had to be carried off on a stretcher babbling and gibbering like an insane baboon, or quivering and twitching like a half-boiled jelly. Of course, it goes without saying really that seeing the laundresses transformed into drooling apes or wobbly desserts was precisely why Cinderella rolled about in the fireplaces in the first place and why she found the practice so utterly enjoyable.

But I'm afraid you haven't heard the worst of it yet, dear reader. Oh no, indeed. You see, the woes of the servants were really nothing. Nothing at all. Not when compared to the suffering of Cinderella's own poor, sweet, darling mother.

Cinderella's mother was kind and gentle and loving and was horrified by her only child's cruel and selfish actions. She would plead with Cinderella to stop rolling in the cinders, to be kind to the servants, and to be respectful to the guests. But Cinderella would only laugh her wicked laugh and skip off to the stables where she could roll about in some horse manure, making the poor laundresses' work that much more stinky and slimy and unbearable.

Then, one day, overcome with despair at Cinderella's meanness and realizing that it was impossible to change her daughter's wicked ways, Cinderella's mother uttered one last remorseful sigh and died on the spot.

At the lavish funeral Cinderella's father held for her mother, Cinderella wailed and moaned and thrashed about, throwing herself down on the floor of the church in a fit of tears, kicking her legs wildly in the air so that one of her shoes went flying off and clonked the unsuspecting priest on the head. Everyone who saw her (with the exception of the priest, who was unconscious) was moved by what they took to be Cinderella's grief at the loss of her mother.

"Poor, unfortunate, kindhearted Cinderella," they would whisper to one another. "She is so distressed by her dear mother's passing. What an angel she is!"

Of course, Cinderella wasn't upset in the least at the loss of her mother's warmth, kindness, and love. Rather, she was sorry that she would no longer have anyone but the servants and guests to tease and torment. She had had such fun torturing her poor mother. And now that fun was over. "Oh, boo hoo, woe is me!" wailed Cinderella, feeling immensely sorry for herself.

When Cinderella's father witnessed the grief of his darling daughter, he decided that he must replace his wife by remarrying as quickly as possible.

And, so, he set out to find an unmarried woman whom he could ask to be his lawfully wedded second wife. As luck would have it, he met just such a woman at the memorial service immediately following the funeral of his dear, departed first wife.

The name of this fortunate woman was Gerlinda and she eagerly accepted Sir Albert's proposal, knowing as she did that Cinderella's father was a wealthy man, as well as a handsome one. Not wanting to waste any time, Gerlinda and Sir Albert married the very next day, and that night Gerlinda moved into her new husband's estate with her two daughters, Gertrude, and Linda.

Cinderella was delighted to make the acquaintance of her new stepsisters and stepmother, thinking that she would now have three family members to torment in place of her one dead mother. Things had turned out wonderfully well for her, as chance would have it.

She tossed her mother's clothes and books out of one of the mansion's windows as a welcoming gesture to her new relatives, but kept her mother's jewelry for herself. The jewelry did, after all, have monetary value and not just silly, worthless sentimental value.

Then, Cinderella set about making the lives of Gerlinda, Gertrude and Linda as miserable as possible.

She began with simple gestures, such as hiding toads, spiders, and snakes in their beds but, unfortunately for her, this game wasn't nearly as much fun as she'd hoped. As it turned out, Gertrude and Linda were animal lovers. They would collect the various insects and reptiles they found in their beds and, rather than screeching in horror and fear as they were supposed to, they would comfort the creatures, helping the poor little snakes and bugs to overcome the shock of being kicked, squished, and squashed when the unsuspecting girls climbed into their beds and sat on them. Once the snakes, spiders, and snails seemed completely recovered from their traumatic ordeal, then the sisters would set them free on the grounds of the estate.

Cinderella was very annoyed by Gertrude's and Linda's lack of distress and dismay, thinking it very selfish of her stepsisters to show so little appreciation for all of her hard work. After all, did they think it was easy or pleasant collecting all of those hideous snakes and nasty bugs? Well, it absolutely wasn't, I can assure you.

She decided that they needed to be punished for their insensitivity towards her ... and she knew just how to make this happen. Oh yes, indeed. She would convince her loving father that her wicked stepmother and ugly stepsisters were forcing her to be their unwilling, unpaid, extremely pretty slave. That would make her dear, doting father absolutely furious. He might even kick Gertrude and Linda and their stupid mother out of the house, replacing them with another wife and stepsiblings who would show more appreciation for her attempts to torture them.

Delighted by her own brilliance, Cinderella leapt high into the air and clicked her heels together in glee. She then set about her work.

She rolled around in the kitchen grate for a while, so that she was covered from head to toe in ashes and soot (which, of course, was nothing new). For added effect, she tore some holes in her dress and then she skipped out to the open-air courtyard that was situated just behind the kitchen. She knew that her father would be arriving home shortly from his daily inspection of the estate's grounds. He would have to pass through the courtyard in order to enter the house.

Well, when he did arrive, he would see his precious little Cinderella, dressed in dirty rags, gathering eggs for her lazy, inconsiderate stepsisters' lunch. That would make him lose his temper, surely.

She laughed her most evil, happy laugh ever and then....

5

"OH, NO!" she fumed to herself, stamping her foot in frustration. "My stupid stepsisters have beaten me to it."

Sure enough, there were Gertrude and Linda standing in the middle of the courtyard, talking to the cook and the stable hand, Edward. The girls had baskets full of eggs dangling from their stepsisterly arms and were wearing plain brown and grey dresses. Their hair was pulled back in simple, modest buns.

"My, but they're ugly," thought Cinderella to herself. "They have no grace, no style. They look like common farm maids. How vile. I certainly hope that their hideousness isn't contagious."

Horrified at just the thought of this revolting possibility, Cinderella gagged and choked and spluttered and spat and hacked and coughed and hootched (whatever that might be).

Startled by the vile and disgusting noises they were hearing, Gertrude, Linda, the cook, and Edward turned in Cinderella's direction.

When the two servants caught sight of her, they immediately ran off as quickly as their legs would carry them. They had been around Cinderella long enough to know that she was probably up to no good. Or, rather, she was DEFINITELY up to no good.

Not having spent enough time with Cinderella to understand just how wicked she could be, however, Gertrude and Linda merely smiled lovingly at their stepsister and called out cheerily, "Why, Cinderella! How wonderful to see you! Have you come to help gather ingredients for today's lunch?"

"Er, yes, as a matter of fact, I have," lied Cinderella, because of course she couldn't very well tell them that she was actually in the courtyard so that her father would think that they had forced her to be their unwilling, unpaid, extremely pretty slave and would, in his fury, boot them both out of the house on their unfashionable backsides.

"That is very kindhearted of you, dear sister," smiled Gertrude. "We have collected enough eggs and were just about to go to the garden to gather some lettuce, tomatoes, and carrots. Would you care to join us?"

"Absolutely not," gasped Cinderella in a shocked voice. "How positively disgusting! What do you think I am … a doltish, good-for-nothing scullery maid?"

Gertrude's and Linda's mouths fell open and their eyes almost popped clean out of their heads and onto the courtyard's cobblestones, they were so surprised to hear their dear, sweet stepsister say such a thing.

When Gertrude finally recovered enough to speak, she stuttered out, "Um … er … perhaps you'd like to take the eggs into the kitchen instead then, dear sister?"

Of course Cinderella wouldn't like this at all. Delivering eggs to mere servants was hardly an appropriate activity for a beautiful, wealthy girl. But, not knowing what else to do, she snatched the baskets of eggs from Gertrude and Linda. When they turned and wandered over to the garden to gather vegetables, she stuck her tongue out at them and then dropped the baskets on the ground, kicking and stomping on the eggs that rolled out of them.

"Well," she said happily to herself, her shoes covered in egg whites and yolks. "That made me feel better! My stupid stepsisters are going to be the death of me. I must think of a less revolting way to get rid of them."

Cinderella thought, plotted, and planned for days and weeks. She was so busy with her scheming that she almost forgot to roll about in the soot and ashes of the estate's fireplaces. But because she wasn't accustomed to using her brain very much, she couldn't come up with a really good, fool-proof, non-revolting plan to destroy her stepsisters and their mother, no matter how hard she tried. Frustrated and upset, she tore angrily at her clothes and her hair until she looked quite a fright. Her golden curls became a frizzy bush of split ends and tangles, sticking out at all kinds of strange and unsightly angles, with lots of bald spots here and there where she had yanked her hair out by its roots. Every single one of her lovely dresses was transformed into tattered rags, and no matter how quickly the dressmaker worked to replace her robes, she couldn't keep up with Cinderella's destructive fingernails. The poor dressmaker finally gave up in despair and keeled over dead, a needle and thread still clutched in her hand.

With the dressmaker dead and gone, Cinderella was forced to wear only rags that tended to fall off in bits as she wandered the halls of her house, thinking and plotting and tearing at her hair. She didn't care. She was too focused on her goal of destroying her stepmother and stepsisters to worry about mere trifles such as clothes and hairdos.

And, if truth be told, she would most likely have ended up without a stitch of clothes on her body and as bald as a ping-pong ball, still roaming about in a very embarrassing, stark-naked fashion, if it hadn't been for a certain royal pronouncement that came out one day.

As luck (good for Cinderella, bad for everyone else) would have it though, she was just in the middle of ripping off one of the sleeves of her few remaining dresses when she overheard her stepmother telling Linda about a ball to be held at the palace of King Snoberatus and Queen Arrogantia the very next night.

"It says here," Gerlinda was saying, her voice breathless with excitement as she studied the parchment that had been delivered to the estate, "that the king and queen are holding a ball to try to find a wife for their son, Prince Charming. Oh, imagine, my dear, what if he was to choose you or Gertrude or Cinderella to be his wife?"

"Oh, he will certainly choose Cinderella over Gertrude or me," said Linda matter-of-factly. "She is so graceful and lovely and beautiful. Gertrude and I look like lumps next to her."

"That's true," thought Cinderella to herself.

"And, anyway, there is already somebody whom I rather like," Linda mumbled shyly, blushing as she did so.

"Why, Linda, who might that be?" asked Gerlinda in surprise, curiosity filling her voice.

"It's Edward, the stable hand," replied Linda, her voice quivering with a mixture of humility and affection. "But, I don't know if he cares for me."

Cinderella didn't hear her stepmother's response to Linda's confession because she was so revolted by her choice of a potential husband. "A stable hand, indeed!" she snorted to herself. "Well, that's probably the best the stupid girl can do, I suppose. But, what I don't understand is how she can actually care about this Edward person. What a complete fool my stepsister is. How I hate her."

Feeling very annoyed at Linda's foolishness, she snatched the parchment announcing the ball from her stepmother's hand and charged off to her bedroom, where she could read it in peace without a bunch of imbeciles milling about.

As she read through the invitation, an idea formed in her frizz-covered, partly bald head.

"I know what I can do!" she thought to herself. "I'll go to this ball and tell the king and queen and prince and all of our neighbors just how horrible my nasty stepsisters and stepmother are to me. Everyone loves me so much ... they're sure to drive my vile relatives out of the kingdom! Oh, how perfect! How brilliant I am! Not to mention gorgeous and beautiful and wonderful!"

She clapped her hands joyfully and did a couple of cartwheels around her bedroom, smashing a mirror and a chair to smithereens in the process.

In the middle of one of her cartwheels though, she suddenly stopped short. A terrible feeling had washed over her.

"I have nothing to wear!" she wailed. "That stupid dressmaker went and died on me and left me nothing but tatters to put on!" She wept loudly, boo-hooing and thrashing around on the floor of her bedroom.

Concerned at the terrible banging and wailing noises Gerlinda heard coming from Cinderella's room, the lady rushed to see what was happening. When she saw Cinderella lying on her bedroom floor, kicking her feet in the air and thumping her fists on the ground, she ran to her to comfort her.

Cinderella bit her on the shin and punched her in the stomach for her pains, but Gerlinda persevered.

"What is the matter, darling?" she said to Cinderella, trying to steer clear of Cinderella's flailing limbs.

"Oh, it is terrible! Awful!" wailed Cinderella. "I have nothing to wear to the ball! Life is so unfair!"

Gerlinda patted Cinderella on the head, being careful to go nowhere near the girl's gnashing, chomping teeth, and then said soothingly, "Why, you can borrow one of your stepsisters' gowns. They won't mind."

Cinderella wailed even louder and thrashed even more wildly at this suggestion. "Oh, how could you suggest such a thing! My stepsisters are big and fat. Their hideous gowns will never fit me! I am so dainty and lovely. I need something befitting of my beauty! Oh, you are breaking my heart!"

Upset and shocked by Cinderella's cruel comments about her daughters—who, while larger than the exceedingly puny Cinderella, were certainly not big and fat (and what would it matter if they were?)—Gerlinda stormed out of Cinderella's bedroom and left her to wallow in her own self pity.

As soon as her stepmother was gone, Cinderella cried all the louder. "Oh, how could she treat me like that! What a cruel woman she is! My real mother would never have been so horrible to me! Oh, why did my mother have to go and leave me to be tormented in this fashion? How I *wish* that she had never left. How I *wish* that she was still here! How I *wish* that she hadn't abandoned me the way that she did."

Now, at the time in which Cinderella lived, if you made a wish three times it invariably came true. So, no sooner had she uttered her third wish than the ghost of her mother appeared before her.

"AAAAAAAAAHHHHHHHHH!" Cinderella screamed. It is always a bit shocking to see a ghost, even when it is the ghost of someone who loved you.

"Hush, dear daughter," said Cinderella's mother in her soft, sweet voice. "You have nothing to fear. I am here in response to your wish."

"Well, it wasn't very considerate of you to scare me the way that you did," grumbled Cinderella grumpily. "I would think that you would be more careful and sensitive. After all, you of all people should know that I have extremely delicate nerves."

Cinderella's mother sighed deeply. But, because her daughter had wished for her to appear, she had no choice but to remain there to see what she wanted. There would be no dying to escape her daughter's nastiness this time around.

Cinderella snapped, "This is no time for sighing and moping about. Seeing as you've barged in upon me so rudely and have most likely traumatized me for life, you might as well do something to make it up to me, the way a good mother should."

Cinderella's mother sighed again. "Yes, dear," she murmured, worried about what terrible deed her daughter might ask her to perform. "What is it that you want?"

"I want to go to the ball at the royal palace tomorrow night," blurted out Cinderella.

Cinderella's mother felt tremendous relief. This didn't sound like a cruel and hurtful request at all. Very unlike Cinderella. Perhaps she had changed.

"And," continued Cinderella, "I need you to make me a dress; the most beautiful dress in the world, befitting of my gorgeousness. And you'll need to fix my hair and give me lots of diamonds and rubies and emeralds to wear, to highlight my delicate features and porcelain complexion. Oh, yes, and I need a carriage and horses to take me to the palace because I don't want to ride with my stupid stepmother and stepsisters and have them crush my dress with their huge, fat behinds."

Cinderella's mother's feeling of relief vanished. Her daughter hadn't changed one bit. She was just as mean as she had ever been. Oh well, at least, Cinderella hadn't asked her to do something dreadful, like turn someone into a toad or make their teeth fall out of their head or expand their nose to the size of a cucumber. Of course, if Cinderella had known that these types of requests would be answered, she would certainly have made them.

11

Fortunately for Gerlinda, Gertrude, and Linda, however, she was completely ignorant of this dangerous fact about wishes.

"Alright, daughter," Cinderella's mother sighed, "your wish is granted," and she raised her hand to provide Cinderella with all that she had requested then and there, on the spot, that very second.

"Not so fast," screeched Cinderella. "I don't want them now, stupid. Come back tomorrow night after my awful stepmother and her two hideous daughters have already left for the ball. I want to surprise them."

Cinderella's mother didn't like to think why such a surprise was important to her daughter, but she could only agree. She had to obey the laws of wishing. She gave one last heartsick sigh, said, "As you wish," and then disappeared.

Cinderella was beside herself with joy. This was far better than she could have hoped. The element of surprise would allow her to catch her stepmother and stepsisters off guard; always a good thing when at war. Not only that, everyone at the ball would assume that Gerlinda and her ghastly daughters had forced her to stay home and miss the ball, just proving how mean and horrible they were to her.

Ah, yes! A brilliant plan, indeed. She clapped her hands delightedly and then she danced around her bedroom, kicking holes in its walls, as she thought about how everyone was going to believe her stepmother and stepsisters were ogres … which, of course, she thought to herself, they absolutely were.

"Oh, I am so brilliant, so fabulous, so wonderful!" she sang, as she whirled and twirled about. "No one is as amazing as me! Oh, la la la, ha ha ha, fa de da de dum!"

That night at dinner and all the next day, Gerlinda, Gertrude, and Linda were amazed at how happy Cinderella seemed.

"Have you decided to go to the ball after all?" asked Gertrude hopefully.

"Oh, no," smiled Cinderella. "No, no. You go ahead without me. I'm just going to stay in and read a book to improve my mind … not that it really needs improving, of course." She skipped off, humming to herself.

"That evil girl is up to no good, mark my words," the head housemaid whispered to the butler as she watched Cinderella's antics and saw her skip off.

"I know, I know," murmured the butler. "Let's just hope nobody dies as a result this time."

They both shook their heads dolefully and prayed that they wouldn't be the target of whatever wicked plan Cinderella was clearly hatching.

When evening rolled around and Sir Albert, Gerlinda, Gertrude, and Linda were ready to set off for the ball, Linda asked Cinderella once more if she wouldn't consider borrowing one of her dresses and joining them.

"Oh no, dear sister," sighed Cinderella, in what was meant to be a piteous, suffering manner. "Your clothes would be far too big and ugly for my delicate frame. Please go ahead without me."

Linda's heart sank at Cinderella's cruel words. She turned and slowly followed her sister, mother, and Sir Albert out to the carriage that was to take them to the palace. She wished that she was staying home. She suddenly felt very plain and frumpy. She would be so out of place at the ball.

Cinderella smiled when she saw Linda's distress.

"My plan is working already," she thought gleefully to herself. "And I have barely begun! Oh, this is surely going to be the best night of my life … and the worst of theirs!"

She dashed eagerly up to her room and shouted out, "Mother! Show yourself! I am ready to go to the ball!"

Her mother's ghost appeared before her, a sad, worried look on her spectral face. She had witnessed Cinderella's cruel treatment of her stepsister and was dreading what her daughter might have in store for her unsuspecting family members.

"Dear…," she began slowly, hoping that she might find just the right words to convince Cinderella to be kind.

"NOT NOW, MOTHER!" snapped Cinderella testily. "I have to get ready for the ball. Can't you see that? Now, do as you promised and make me a fabulous dress and fix my hair and cover me in precious jewels."

She stood before her poor dead mother, who had no choice but to fulfill her daughter's wishes. Just as well, really, as she couldn't think of anything to say that might convince Cinderella to be kind. That was truly an impossible task.

She asked Cinderella to close her eyes and then, only moments later, she told her that she could open them and take a look at herself.

When Cinderella gazed upon her reflection in the mirror, she was pleased to see that her mother had done a fairly decent job. Her dress was designed in the fashion of the day, with a pinched waist and a large, billowing skirt that fell to the floor, a long train trailing behind it. It was woven out of pure silver and gold thread, and glittered and glinted when Cinderella moved about to admire herself at various angles. Her hair had been de-frizzed, de-tangled, and de-balded, and was piled high on her head in a mountain of silky, shiny, cascading curls. Diamonds and rubies dripped from her ears and her throat. Silver slippers graced her dainty feet.

"Hmmmm," Cinderella murmured, her head cocked to one side as she considered her reflection. "Not bad. I need more jewels though. And these shoes are so last season. I want something really special. And hurry up about it. The ball has already started."

Cinderella's mother sighed for the umpteenth time and then, asking her daughter to close her eyes once more, she went back to work. When she was finished, Cinderella opened her eyes and was delighted to see that she was now literally covered in diamonds. They sparkled in her golden curls and were sprinkled throughout the fabric of her dress. She even had two at either corner of her eyes, setting off their wonderful, silvery blue color.

She pulled up the hem of her skirt to inspect her shoes and was pleased to see that the silver shoes had been replaced by high-heeled glass slippers. No one else had anything like these!

"This will do," she said ungraciously. "Lucky for you, I am a natural beauty. Made your job pretty easy, all in all."

Cinderella's mother said nothing. After all, what could be said?

"Okay," Cinderella said impatiently. "This is no time for staring off into space. I have to get to the ball. Make me my carriage. And provide me with some footmen while you're at it. I must arrive in style."

She dashed off down the massive circular staircase to the entrance hall, followed by her mother's ghost, and threw open the front door to the house.

"Let's go, let's go," urged Cinderella, tapping her little glass-shod foot. "What are you waiting for?"

Cinderella's mother replied wearily, "We must go to the garden, so I can collect what I need for the spell."

"The garden?!!" shrieked Cinderella. "That seems an awfully stupid place to gather what is needed for my carriage. But if you must go there, well then you must. I'm staying here though. It would be ridiculous for me to go traipsing about in all that muck in my lovely new ball gown and slippers."

Cinderella's mother looked sadly at her selfish daughter and then turned and moved in the direction of the garden.

"Hurry up, while you're about it!" shouted Cinderella from the doorway. "You've already made me late for the ball."

When Cinderella's mother arrived at the garden, she looked around for things she might use to create a carriage, horses, and footmen.

When she spotted a large orange pumpkin, she knew that she had the perfect ingredients for the carriage. She touched it. It shimmered and shuddered for a moment and then, suddenly—poof!—it was transformed into a golden coach that glinted in the moonlight.

Next for the horses. For them, Cinderella's mother selected four white mice. She stroked the soft fur on their tiny backs; and then they, like the pumpkin, were suddenly transformed. They stood before her... four prancing white horses.

Three rats that were gnawing on carrots, lettuce, and broccoli in the garden would do very nicely for the coachman and two footmen. When they materialized, they were dressed in grey livery, with rather unseemly, long, wiry whiskers and the odd bit of vegetable stuck to them here and there. Ah, well. Nothing is perfect.

The footmen and the coachman awaited Cinderella's mother's instructions about what they were to do.

Cinderella's mother hesitated for a moment. She knew in her heart that Cinderella was up to no good. She didn't know exactly what her daughter had planned for the evening, but she was sure that something dreadful was going to happen at the ball. Because of the laws of wishing, she had had no choice but to grant her daughter's requests, but perhaps there was a way that she could limit the damage Cinderella might be planning on doing.

She thought and thought, and then, just as she heard Cinderella yelling out angrily for her to "hurry up, why don't you?" an idea came to her.

She would tell Cinderella that the magic would only last until midnight, and then everything would return to its original state. Cinderella wouldn't want to be caught dead at a ball in her tattered dress and frizzy, patchy hair. She would certainly leave the ball before the clock struck twelve.

It was already nine o'clock. This meant that Cinderella would only have three hours in which to wreak havoc. Not ideal, but better than the alternative ... which was, of course, no limit whatsoever to what Cinderella might do.

Cinderella's mother turned to the coachman and the footmen and instructed them to drive up to the front door of the house, where they would collect Cinderella and transport her to the ball. When they arrived at the front of the house, Cinderella was standing on the top step, fuming.

"Well!" she snarled. "That took much longer than I might have hoped. You have made me tremendously late for the ball. I hope you're happy about that."

Actually, Cinderella's mother *was* happy about that; extremely happy about that.

Cinderella pushed past the footmen who were planning on helping her into the carriage and jumped in herself. Before she could order the coachman to drive off, Cinderella's mother blurted out, "I must tell you, daughter, that the magic will only last until midnight. You must leave the ball before the clock strikes twelve, or you will find yourself there in your tattered gown." She decided not to mention the frizzy hair bit, thinking that this would only infuriate Cinderella and make her even meaner than usual.

Cinderella grumbled, "Well, that stinks, I must say. Thanks for nothing." She ordered the coachman not to waste another minute and to drive off to the royal palace.

Her last words to her mother, as the carriage shot away, were, "And the servants you got for me are absolutely hopeless. They smell like carrots and broccoli."

When Cinderella got to the palace, she composed her features so that she would look like the charming and sweet angel she wanted—and completely expected—everyone to believe her to be. She sailed gracefully up the front steps where she was greeted by the royal family's head manservant. He escorted her to the ballroom, where he announced her arrival to the guests who were already there.

When the men and women who filled the ballroom turned to look at Cinderella, they were amazed by her beauty and let out a loud series of "oohs," "ahhhs," and "well, I nevers."

"She is spectacular!" gasped one man.

"Glorious!" said another.

"Who is that beauteous angel?" exclaimed the prince, completely mesmerized.

"Perfect!" snorted Cinderella smugly to herself. "The impression has been made! Everyone sees me for the wonderful, gorgeous, sweet, fabulous person I am. They are going to be horrified when they hear how cruelly I have been treated by my evil stepmother and ugly stepsisters! Which reminds me, where are those hags anyway?"

She looked around and was pleased to see the astonished looks on her family members' faces at the sight of her. Her pleasure soon turned to annoyance, however, when Gertrude and Linda rushed over to her, throwing their arms around her in a warm, welcoming, un-haglike embrace.

"They are going to completely spoil the impression I'm trying to make," she grumbled to herself. "Stupid fools. They're wrecking everything!"

But she hugged them back, as any angelic sister would. "I must think, I must think," she mused to herself. "There must be some way to fix the mess these dolts have made of my brilliant plans. Ooh, how I hate them!"

Trying to control her urge to punch Gertrude and Linda in their heads, she smiled sweetly and fakely at her stepsisters, who whispered excitedly, "We must take you to meet Prince Charming! Did you hear what he said when you came in? 'A beauteous angel,' no less! We met him earlier this evening. He's simply lovely. And he is going to adore you!"

Cinderella reluctantly agreed to allow her stepsisters to lead her over to the prince, fuming at the way they were ruining her plans for the evening. The prince was going to think that Gertrude and Linda were actually kind to her at this rate. Preposterous! They were beasts! "Oh well," she thought. "At least I'll look especially beautiful next to the two of them."

Before Gertrude and Linda could lead her over to where Prince Charming had been standing just a moment before, he had leapt across the room and had landed with a thud at Cinderella's side.

"Oh, my glorious, spectacular, splendiforous vision of loveliness," he exclaimed. "You must absolutely, positively, undeniably, definite-ootly dance with me!"

Cinderella put on her best fake, shy, and modest smile and curtseyed. "Oh, while I am so undeserving of such an honor and such charming compliments, of course I will dance with you if you so command it of me, your highness," she simpered.

"I do!" he blurted out. "And I always get my way!"

Actually, this was absolutely true. Prince Charming had been raised to believe he was the most wonderful, most important person in the world. He expected everyone to do exactly as he ordered and would have them beheaded if they disobeyed him. Another one of his many charming characteristics was his love of playing clever little tricks on people, like pulling chairs out from under them so that they would fall to the floor and crack their skulls. Everyone would laugh uproariously when he carried out a prank of this kind ... even the person with the cracked skull. They had no choice, really, because they would be beheaded if they didn't laugh. Needless to say, this endearing trait of his had gained the prince the reputation of being a fun-loving, humorous young man. It was no wonder that most of the young women in the kingdom were eager to catch his eye and to be his bride.

There was also the matter of his being exceedingly rich and handsome too, of course. But these facts would hardly have turned a young woman's head if it wasn't for his pleasant, carefree personality.

When Prince Charming led Cinderella onto the dance floor, all of the ball guests stood and gazed upon them, completely enraptured. With the exception of the girls who had hoped that they might one day be married to the prince themselves, everyone was awestruck by the beauty of the glorious couple. They danced together all evening, the prince occasionally sticking out his foot to trip up another dancer, much to the amusement of Cinderella and the other guests.

Cinderella whispered eagerly, "Trip my ugly stepsisters. Trip them up, too!"

The prince was delighted that Cinderella was a creature after his own heart with an equally endearing sense of humor. "This is a young lady I might consider marrying," he thought. "We could have some fun together."

The next time Linda waltzed by, Prince Charming obligingly stuck out his foot to trip her up. When she toppled to the ground, Gertrude rushed over to help her sister. Prince Charming took this wonderful opportunity to kick Gertrude in the backside and send her tumbling over on top of her sister.

Cinderella couldn't have been more thrilled. "I think I'll marry this man," she mused. "I can see that we could be very happy together."

Completely smitten by one another's delightful qualities, Cinderella and the prince gazed lovingly into each other's eyes. They might even have kissed if, just then, Cinderella hadn't suddenly heard the clock begin to strike twelve.

"Oh, drat!" she blurted out. "I must go!" There was no way that she was going to let the prince see her without all of her finery.

She dashed towards the door, with the prince in hot pursuit.

"Where are you going, my darling, lovely, beauteous, precious angel?" he cried out.

"No time to talk!" she panted as she sprinted towards home. The high-heeled glass slippers seriously slowed her progress, and the prince might have caught up with her if she hadn't tugged them off her feet, grumbling, "Stupid things! Why couldn't my hopeless mother have come up with something more practical!" She threw the slippers away angrily, accidentally clonking the prince on the head with one of them as she did so, rendering him unconscious.

"Perfect," she muttered when she saw him sprawled on the ground. "Now I can definitely get home without him catching up to me."

When she arrived back at her own estate, breathless and sweaty, she was flabbergasted to see that she was still wearing the lovely gown, in spite of her ghost-mother's ominous warning.

"Why! My mother lied to me!" she blurted out furiously. "How dare she! And now I can't go back to the ball, because I'm all sweaty … and the prince is either unconscious or dead. Oh, how I hate her! She has ruined my life!"

Cinderella burst into self-pitying tears and ran up to her bedroom. Tearing off her gown, she flung herself on her bed where she could thrash around furiously without hurting herself. When she had kicked, screamed, wailed, and screeched for two hours or so, she finally fell asleep, utterly exhausted by her outburst.

She slept for twelve hours, snoring loudly, and, when she awoke, she could see that her tantrum of the night before had transformed her golden hair from a mass of shiny curls into a freakish, patchy bush once more.

Grumbling, she tossed on one of her many tattered gowns.

"Everyone is so horrible to me," she muttered under her breath. "Even the prince couldn't be bothered to follow me here, the brute." He *was* unconscious, or dead, when she had left him, but, nonetheless … that was really no excuse.

She stomped angrily downstairs to the dining room, where her family was seated around the large oak table eating a late lunch.

Gertrude jumped up out of her chair and darted over to Cinderella.

"Dear sister," she exclaimed, her voice filled with affection and concern, "what happened to you last night? Everyone was so worried about you. When we couldn't find you, we rushed home only to find you asleep in your bed. Why did you leave without us? Did something happen?"

"And did you hear about Prince Charming?" interrupted Linda excitedly. "Someone knocked him unconscious with a glass slipper, clearly in an attempt to murder him! He remembers nothing of the attack or about the ball, but a search is going to be conducted to find the owner of the offending attempted-murder slipper."

"Uh oh," gulped Cinderella to herself, "I'd better lie low." Out loud she murmured in her best fake sick-person voice, "I'm afraid I'm not feeling well. That's why I left the ball early. In fact, I'm still not feeling well, so I think I'll go back up to bed."

She grabbed a whole roast chicken, a hunk of cheese, and a loaf of bread to take with her—because of course a two-hour tantrum would make anyone ravenously hungry—and then dashed back up to her room. No sooner had she begun stuffing the food into her mouth than she heard her father calling her.

"Cinderella," he shouted from the ground floor, "you must come down at once. The prince is here and every member of the household is ordered to appear before him."

"But I'm not well, father," wailed Cinderella, spewing half-chewed food about her room.

"You'll feel less well if he beheads you for failing to follow his orders," replied her father impatiently.

Cinderella had no choice but to stomp back downstairs. For the first time in her life, she trembled with fear. What if the prince discovered that the slipper belonged to her? Would she be arrested? Would she be executed? How dreadful! She was far too beautiful and lovely and perfect to be dead or in prison!

When she arrived in the front hall, her father, stepmother, and stepsisters were lined up before the prince and two of his footmen.

The prince was waving Cinderella's glass slipper around in his hand.

"Who tried to kill me with this dangerous weapon?" he was demanding. "Who would commit such a vile and savage act of treason?"

When no one answered, he continued. "Well, if no one will own up to this dastardly crime, there is nothing for it but to try the slipper on each one of you to see if it fits. I'll begin with you, sir," he said to Cinderella's father.

He tried to jam the slipper onto each person's foot, beginning with Sir Albert, stubbing their toes and chafing their skin in the process. But, being about the size of a doll's shoe, the slipper was far too tiny for any of them.

When he got to Cinderella, she blurted out nervously, "You won't want to try it on my foot, dear, wonderful, forgiving, non-beheading prince. I have bunions and fungus and a terrible case of athlete's foot. I fear you might catch these horrible diseases yourself."

"No worries," replied the prince. "I'll have one of my footmen try it on you."

The footman knelt down and slipped the shoe on Cinderella's perfectly healthy foot.

"She is the one, your highness!" exclaimed the footman. "She is the only person who has a puny enough foot to fit this doll-sized slipper."

"Well, I never!" blurted out Cinderella, so offended by the man's insulting "puny" comment that she hardly cared that she had just been unmasked as the perpetrator of the attack against the prince.

When Prince Charming saw the slipper on Cinderella's foot, his memory of the night before returned to him like a lightning bolt from the blue … or, rather, like a glass slipper from the sky.

"My angel!" he exclaimed. "My cootchy-coo, my sweetie-pie, my tweedle-dee-dee!" He fell to his knees before Cinderella and said, "You must become my wife! It is an order!"

Cinderella smiled her most un-Cinderella-like, sweet smile and replied, "Of course, my darling prince."

"We'll get married tomorrow!" he burst out excitedly.

"But I have nothing to wear!" she whined. "Do you see the rags my family forces me to wear?" She twirled around so that he could take in the full terribleness of her outfit … as well as her dainty figure.

"Horrendous! Shocking!" he said. "Shall I have them beheaded?"

Cinderella's father, stepmother, and stepsisters shot pleading, desperate looks at Cinderella, begging her with their round, terrified eyes to spare their lives.

"Ummmm," she considered. "Well, let's see ... er ... no, perhaps not. By choosing not to have them beheaded, in spite of all of the horrible things they've done to me, I will prove to all of the citizens of the kingdom that I am a wonderful, loving, forgiving person."

"Oh, and so you are, my love!" the prince exclaimed, spitting on Cinderella in his excitement. "I have never met anyone as wonderful as you, I must say, except for myself, of course!" He then added, "I'll have the royal dressmakers stay up all night to make you a new wardrobe befitting of a princess. That way, we can marry tomorrow and you can get away from these cruel, despicable people with whom you now live."

"Wonderful!" she smiled. Her plan had worked out perfectly after all. Her family had been exposed for the nasty, awful people that they were, and she had gotten herself a prince in the process. This was far, far better than she could ever have wished!

Now, dear reader, you might assume that once Cinderella and Prince Charming were married, they then proceeded to live happily ever after. This, I'm pleased to say, was not the case in this completely true recounting of their life story.

Because, naturally, being completely selfish and wicked people, Cinderella and Prince Charming grew to despise one another more and more as time went by (about one week after the wedding, to be exact). They would call each other terrible names like "poo-poo-head" and "wombat breath," and would kick each other in the shins at least once an hour. Prince Charming ordered the servants to behead Cinderella on a regular basis. Cinderella, for her part, had learned that she only had to knock the prince unconscious with a shoe or a vase or something similarly heavy in order to make him forget that he had issued such an order. And so, in their way, they learned to live together. And were perfectly, completely, utterly miserable.

Kindhearted Linda, in the meantime, grew more and more beautiful with the passing of the years, as all sweet-tempered people do. It is a law of nature, you see, that as you get older, your inside always shows up on your outside. It wasn't long before her gorgeousness surpassed anything that Cinderella could—and did—ever boast of, especially because, as Linda became prettier, Cinderella's meanness started gobbling up her nasty little face until she became as ugly as a gnome. The beautiful Linda married her beloved stable hand, Edward. Unlike Cinderella and her prince, Linda and Edward did indeed live happily ever after, raising countless children and an even more countless number of chickens, pigs, and horses.

"And what about Gertrude?" you might well ask. "What happened to her?"

Well, the good-natured, and now spectacularly lovely, Gertrude became a veterinarian and traveled to Africa, where she had plenty of wild beasts, venomous reptiles, poisonous insects, and other deadly creatures to keep her happy. It goes without saying that she was exceedingly pleased to live in such a safe environment after the time she had spent with Cinderella.

The End

If your head is something you'd like to keep,
make sure you're not a vain, mean creep.

Little Red Riding Hood

Once upon a time, in a land far, far away, there lived a charming, sweet, generous girl named Rebecca.

Sadly, she is not the Rebecca of this story.

Oh no. Far from it.

The Rebecca in this woeful tale was anything but charming and sweet and generous. She was, if truth be told, the meanest, nastiest, most selfish brute who ever lived in the place that she lived, at the time that she lived there.

More than anything else, Rebecca loved to see other creatures suffer. If she spotted a little bird with a broken wing lying in the garden of her family's enormous estate, she would chuckle with merriment. If she stepped on a ladybug, squashing it flat, she would split her sides laughing. But, oh my goodness, nothing made her happier than watching people and animals come begging for food at her family's beautiful home. These poor starving creatures would plead on bended knee for a crust of bread or a drop of water.

But, they got none of it. Not one crumb. Not one atom.

You see, Rebecca's parents, Lord and Lady Tightwad, were every bit as cruel, miserly, and horrible as their selfish daughter. They would kick the pitiful beggars to send them on their way and then, as the poor, desperate folks shuffled back to their hovels in the woods, Lord and Lady Tightwad would shout at their departing backs: "Be off with you, you lazy, useless louts. If you ever show your worthless faces here again, we'll rip out your tongues and yank out your rotten, yellow teeth. You won't be wanting bread then, we can assure you!"

Oh, how this made Rebecca roar with laughter! She would roll about on the front lawn, her shiny brown curls flopping this way and that, her sparkling violet eyes spinning around with glee, and her squidgy little stomach aching with the tremendous joy that bubbled up inside of her.

Lord and Lady Tightwad loved to see their daughter so deliriously, deliciously happy. She was the only person in the world, besides themselves, whom they didn't want to be utterly miserable. They would smile down at her as she rolled about in the grass and would say tenderly, "We know something that will make you laugh even louder, sweet little chickadee."

Then Rebecca's parents would snap their fingers at one of their many servants, who would scuttle off to gather up all of the slabs of roast beef and loaves of freshly baked bread and mashed potatoes, honeyed carrots, pies, and cakes that Rebecca and her parents hadn't been able to finish at lunch that day. The servant would make a mountain of this food on the mansion's front lawn and would then throw a few logs and sticks on the pile before setting the whole mess on fire.

The smell of the burning food would carry on the wind, filling the nostrils of the starving men, women, children, and animals who lived in the surrounding woods, making their stomachs rumble with hunger and their hearts ache with despair.

And mixed in with the smell of the food was always the sound of Rebecca's delighted tinkling laughter. "Oh, how wonderful it is to be me!" she would think to herself. "Life is such fun!"

Still chuckling happily, she would trot upstairs to her bedroom to enjoy a much-deserved afternoon nap under the soft silk sheets of her four-poster feather bed. "It is such hard, tiring work putting other people in their proper place," she would yawn. And then she would fall asleep to dreams of squashed bugs and hungry peasants. These dreams always made her feel very content. She would wake from them thinking, "I have so much more than everybody else. I am truly a very special, wonderful person!" and she would bounce downstairs to the dining room for a delicious afternoon tea of tiny little vanilla cakes, strawberry tarts, and chocolate éclairs.

"I wonder what the beggars are eating right now?" she would ask her parents in a joking manner, and they would all laugh at her charming sense of humor because, why, of course the beggars were eating nothing at all, except perhaps leaves, dirt, and caterpillars.

Life carried on very merrily this way for the Tightwad family until one fine day when a messenger on horseback arrived at the house and knocked loudly on the front door.

"KNOCK! KNOCK!"

"Who's there?" bellowed the butler from inside the mansion.

"A messenger," answered the messenger impatiently.

"A messenger who?" shouted the butler through the door.

"Stop clowning around, you old fool, and let me in!" yelled the messenger angrily.

When the butler opened the door, the messenger blurted out, "I have a message from old Lady Tightwad for her son, Lord Tightwad; and here it is." He thrust a slip of paper in the butler's hand and then jumped on his horse and galloped off as fast as he could. He didn't want to chance an encounter with the horrible Lord and Lady Tightwad and their miserable daughter. Every encounter ended in pain, misery, and a kick in the shins.

The butler shuffled off to the parlor in which the Tightwads were busy doing nothing at all but lounging about.

"A message for Lord Tightwad from the venerable old Lady Tightwad," boomed the butler, who was quite deaf and thus always spoke in a very loud voice so he might know what he was saying.

"You don't need to yell, you stupid man," roared back Lord Tightwad. "*We're* not deaf, you know." He snatched the message from the butler's grasp and read through it.

"Hmmm," he muttered. "Old mater isn't feeling too well. Seems she's stubbed her toe. Terrible, terrible. She wants us to pay her a visit to raise her spirits."

"Well, I'm not going," yawned Lady Tightwad. "I'm far too busy." She quickly fell asleep on the couch on which she was lying.

"Yes, well, I'm too busy, too," grumbled Lord Tightwad, whose eyes were about to close themselves.

"I'll go! I'll go!" trilled Rebecca. She loved visiting her grandmother because old Lady Tightwad lived in a sweet little cottage in the woods. Now, you might be wondering why a wealthy lady like her would want to live in a cottage … in the woods no less. Well, it was quite simple really. The forest was filled with poor, hungry people and starving, desperate animals, and because she lived so close to them, old Lady Tightwad was able to torture them on a daily basis with the lip-smacking scent of baking that was constantly wafting through her kitchen window… baking that was done specifically for tormenting purposes, not for eating purposes as you might have imagined. Old Lady Tightwad actually hated cakes, pies, and anything that was sweet, and she never let them near her lips … or any other part of her. She was very odd that way. But that didn't matter. Everything that her cook baked for her just ended up in the fireplace anyway, burned to bits. And, of course, the smell of scorched pastries tortured the poor, starving peasants and animals that much more.

All of this wonderful teasing delighted dear little Rebecca who loved to watch her grandmother shovel platefuls of delectable goodies onto the fire. She even got to eat some of the cookies, cakes, and pastries herself because, unlike old Lady Tightwad, Rebecca loved sugary treats.

And so, she was naturally very anxious to be given the chance to visit her fun-loving grandmother.

Rebecca bounced up and down and pleaded with her father, "Please let me go, dear Papa. I so long to cheer up Grandmama!"

"Alright then," her father mumbled, falling asleep with his mouth wide open in a loud snore.

"Spectacular!" exclaimed Rebecca. "Lots of treats for me to eat, and hundreds of peasants to torture while I'm at it. Stupendous! I'm going to set out right away."

She changed into her visiting dress of finest violet silk and then grabbed the red velvet riding cloak with the peaked hood, which her grandmother had given her for her last birthday. "I'll wear this," smiled Rebecca to herself. "That will put Grandmama in an extra good mood, which means bad news for all of those lazy animals and people lying about in the woods doing nothing but grumble about their empty stomachs when they should be busy slaving away for people like me."

She wrapped the cloak around her shoulders and pulled the hood over her shiny brown curls and, then, off she went, skipping lickety-split to her grandmother's cottage.

When she entered the woods, she came across many pitifully thin people and animals who begged her weakly for a little food. "I have nothing on me; can't you see you dumb twerps?" she snapped back, kicking out at them with her little leather boots. "Get away before I send my father, Lord Tightwad after you." As soon as they heard the name Tightwad, the beggars fainted dead away or ran screaming into the deepest, darkest depths of the woods.

"Hah! Hah! Hah!" roared Rebecca in her little red riding hood. "What cowards they all are! Frightened of a sweet, innocent little thing like me!"

She skipped along some more until she came across a wolf with three little wolf pups on the path.

"Out of my way!" snarled Rebecca. "I'm a very important person going to see another very important person."

"Oh, please, little Miss Red Riding Hood," pleaded the wolf. "My pups are starving. If they don't get food soon, they'll die. Please can you spare something, anything."

"No!" shouted Rebecca. "I can't. I don't have any food. Isn't that obvious, you fool? And my name isn't Red Riding Hood, stupid. Why on earth would you think it was?" She crossed her arms angrily under her red velvet cape.

The wolf hung her head dejectedly.

Suddenly, a cruel, nasty plan popped into Rebecca's hood-covered head.

"About that food," she said, a scheming smile creasing her wicked face, "while I don't have any with me, I am on my way to see someone who has loads and piles and mountains of food … enough for you and your mangy babies. Why don't you come with me and see for yourself?"

The wolf looked up at Rebecca and gasped gratefully, "Oh that would be wonderful, dear Miss Red Riding Hood. It's not really for me, you understand. Just my little pups."

"Well, come with me then," said Rebecca, delighted that her plan was working so well. "And stop calling me Red Riding Hood. I hate that name. It's ridiculous."

"Oh, I will, I will stop! I promise!" gushed the wolf. "And thank you! Thank you so much, Miss Red Riding Hood!" She trotted after Rebecca as the little pups scrambled behind on their trembling, skinny legs.

When they arrived at old Lady Tightwad's house, Rebecca turned to the wolf and demanded bossily, "You just wait here. My grandmother lives in this charming cottage. I'll ask her to have her cook make some wonderful goodies."

The wolf bowed her head and whispered, "I will never be able to thank you enough. You are saving our lives."

"That's right," Rebecca said, smiling her wicked, scheming smile again. "So, anyway, about that food … how does rack of lamb with mint sauce and freshly baked bread, and roast potatoes and cherry pie sound to you?"

The pups all began drooling and yipping with excitement.

"Wonderful! Like heaven!" whispered the wolf reverently, almost too overwhelmed with gratitude to speak.

"Marvelous," grinned Rebecca. "We'll begin with those then, shall we?"

She knocked on the door, and her grandmother's butler let her in.

"Grandmama," shrieked Rebecca, knocking the butler to the floor and running to give old Lady Tightwad a big hug.

"My darling child!" exclaimed the grandmother. "It is so wonderful for you to come! My toe is simply killing me."

"Poor you!" said Rebecca, not caring about her grandmother's toe one whit and not so much as glancing its way. "Let's eat."

"Wouldn't you like to chat a bit first?" asked old Lady Tightwad. "I so love hearing about all of the cute little pranks you play on people. Such a clever girl, you are. And I wanted to show you these charming, new gold-rimmed spectacles I just purchased—so sophisticated—and my glorious, new grey wig that truly highlights my breathtaking beauty, I must say." She patted what looked for all the world like an old, dead cat sitting on her head.

"No, no," replied Rebecca impatiently. "I've walked at least half a mile to get here. I'm starving. I must eat."

"Alright then, dear," chuckled her grandmother, patting the dead cat. "I'll have Cook make something for us quick as a wink."

"I want rack of lamb with mint sauce, freshly baked bread, roast potatoes, and cherry pie," blurted out Rebecca, without pausing to so much as take a breath.

"Well, I'll see if she can manage to make those…," began old Lady Tightwad.

"She must! She must!" screamed Rebecca, stamping her little leather boots on the stone floor of the cottage.

"So she must," smiled the grandmother. "My, you're turning into a fine young lady."

The grandmother gave the cook the orders for lunch and, because the cook was a witch who could rustle up meals in no time flat, the food was on the table in mere minutes.

"Open the dining room window while we eat," Rebecca ordered her grandmother.

"Oh, I don't know, dear," said her grandmother anxiously. "It's a bit drafty out. I must take care of my toe."

"But I want all of the peasants to smell what we're eating," whined Rebecca.

"Oh my, oh my! Why didn't you say so in the first place," laughed old Lady Tightwad. "Of course we'll open the window. What a treat it will be to hear them all moaning and groaning with hunger. It will make the food seem all the more delicious, knowing that they can't have any. Cook, open the window!" she roared in the direction of the kitchen.

Once the window had been opened, Rebecca peered out of it. Sure enough there was the wolf and her three little pups, waiting patiently outside.

"Perfect," chortled Rebecca to herself. "Let's eat, Grandmama!" she said in a loud voice that even the deaf old butler could probably hear way back at her family's mansion. "Yummm … rack of lamb and mint sauce, roast potatoes, freshly baked bread, and delicious cherry pie for dessert. My favorite!"

They ate and ate and ate. She could hear the little wolf puppies whimpering with hunger outside.

When they had eaten every last scrap on the table, with much smacking of lips and extra loud "yum-yumming," she said to her grandmother, "Now let's have some roast beef with Yorkshire pudding and green beans and a chocolate cake for dessert."

"My, you are hungry, dear," smiled the grandmother. "I don't think I can eat another bite myself."

"But you must, you absolutely must!" screeched Rebecca. "I will be so sad if you don't!"

"Alright then, dear," said old Lady Tightwad, who actually liked an excuse to stuff herself silly. "But you'll have to eat all of the cake for dessert, just as you ate all of the cherry pie. You know I don't like sweet treats."

"I will! I will!" sang Rebecca, bouncing up and down in her seat.

In a twinkling, the second lunch was on the table. By now, Rebecca could hear the wolf's and wolf pups' stomachs rumbling loudly.

"This is so perfect!" laughed Rebecca to herself. "That stupid wolf and her babies must be going absolutely crazy. This is truly the funniest, best joke ever!"

She and her grandmother stuffed every last morsel down their throats without even stopping to chew, and then Rebecca urged, "Again, again! I need more food! More food!"

The cook whipped up pork sausages with baked beans, hot biscuits, and lemon tarts, and those too were soon gone. Then there was roast turkey with stuffing and cranberry sauce, mashed potatoes with warm butter, peas, and fruit cake with marzipan icing. Next came a large steaming ham with mustard dressing, scalloped potatoes, broccoli, and strawberry shortcake.

This went on all afternoon, with Rebecca and her grandmother's stomachs growing bigger and bigger. They hardly even knew what they were putting in their mouths as they didn't stop to think … or chew. They just shoved whole sausages and chunks of ham, turkey, and roast beef, and slices of cake right down their throats, like a couple of big pythons swallowing herds of elephants, wildebeests, and zebras in one giant gulp.

Outside, the poor wolf was trying to comfort her three little pups who were beginning to faint with hunger. "Don't worry, dears, your food will be coming soon," she whispered. "That little girl promised. It won't be long now."

And, you know, she was right.

For, all of a sudden, there were two tremendously loud popping noises, "POP! POP!", and roast beef, broccoli, pork sausages, roast turkey, stuffing, cranberry sauce, rack of lamb, mashed potatoes, carrots, green beans, roast potatoes, lemon tarts, strawberry shortcake, cherry pie, freshly baked bread, hot biscuits, and chocolate cake came flying out the window.

"She remembered! She remembered!" squealed the pups excitedly, and they started gobbling up all of the wonderful food that had flown their way.

"She even gave us her lovely red riding cape to keep us all warm," marveled the wolf with tears in her eyes, as Rebecca's cape came hurtling out, along with a piece of pie and a slab of roast beef. "How kind. I will think of little Miss Red Riding Hood every time I see it."

"And she gave us her sweet leather boots as well," chimed in one of the pups, as Rebecca's boots landed with a plop in the grass.

"And a pair of gold spectacles and a grey wig," added the second pup, as they too hit the ground.

"I think that's a dead cat," said the third pup.

The wolf looked at the wig, glasses, boots, and cape, and all of the food that lay strewn about them, and she wept with happiness. "I have never met such kindhearted, generous people, truly I haven't," she whispered.

And she never would in future, because, of course, Rebecca and her grandmother were never to be seen nor heard of again.

When the witch who worked in old Lady Tightwad's kitchen peeked into the dining room to see what the popping was all about and saw that the old woman and her granddaughter had disappeared, she rushed outside and exclaimed, "Thank you, dear wolf, for rescuing me from my servitude! I have been a prisoner of old Lady Tightwad for longer than I can even remember, ever since I was a little witch girl and she offered my loving parents a gold coin and a basket of boiled eggs if they would sell me to her. Please let me repay your kindness by allowing me to become your humble, devoted servant, so that I may cook you a feast every day for the rest of your lives."

The pups tumbled over themselves with joy and the wolf wept her biggest tears yet.

And, so it came to pass that the wolf and her pups led a wonderful life with mountains of food to eat each day, which they shared with all of the other poor people and animals who lived in the forest. Nobody ever had to go hungry again.

And everyone lived happily ever after, except Rebecca's parents, who had no one left to tease and torment once the peasants stopped knocking on the door of their grand mansion begging for a scrap of bread or a drop of water.

Oh, yes, and except for Rebecca and her grandmother too, of course, because … well, you know what happened to them.

POP! POP!

The End

If you don't want to go POP, POP,
be kind to those without a lot.

The Three Little Pigs

Long ago, when animals could still speak and had a tendency to dress up in charming sailor suits, bonnets, and such-like to hide their nakedness, there lived three little pigs ... who, if truth be told, were anything but little.

Being extremely greedy, self-indulgent creatures, their bodies had expanded to enormous proportions. They could hardly fit into their sailor suits, and over time they had burst numerous seams and popped countless buttons. They didn't much care about this sad state of their attire, however, because, in addition to being extraordinarily greedy and self-indulgent, they were also quite slovenly and tasteless.

No matter.

The pigs, who were brothers, went by the names of Percival, Archibald, and Charlemagne, or Percy, Archie, and Charley for short. They lived together in a dilapidated house which Percy had built of straw; a very simple structure that had been quick and easy to build, laziness being yet another charming trait of the three pigs.

Archie and Charley, the two eldest pigs, believed that everyone and everything had been put on Earth for their personal pleasure and profit, and anyone who didn't see things this way, well, really didn't deserve to live.

And so, it came to pass that on a certain Tuesday morning, while Archie was reading *The Piglet Times*, he stumbled across a piece of news that would change the course of history for him and his brothers forever.

"Listen up boys," Archie squealed excitedly.

"What?" grunted Charley grumpily, spraying bits of half-chewed food across the table. "This had better be good. I'm in the middle of something important." Indeed he was. He was just about to poke Percy in the eye with a fork, a joke of which the pigs were very fond. They loved practical jokes of all kinds; such as setting each other's tails on fire, knocking one another unconscious with logs, bricks, and old shin bones, and gluing each other's rather large behinds to the toilet seat. The more painful the joke, the more they enjoyed it.

And, if they treated each other this way, dear reader, you can only imagine how they treated all of the people and animals whom they didn't particularly like ... which was basically everyone in the world besides themselves... at least as far as Archie and Charley were concerned.

Archie continued. "This is good. I promise you!"

He proceeded to read aloud an announcement that proclaimed:

"Hear ye! Hear ye! Ye are hereby informed that the king and queen of our fair land will be taking up residence for the summer months in the Palace of Liberatas. All citizens of the land are forthwith invited to pay their respects to the venerable royal family, if they should so desire. A representative of the royal family will call upon each citizen of the kingdom over the coming days to issue an invitation in person."

"Isn't this fantastic!" squealed Archie excitedly.

"No. Not really," replied Charley in a bored voice, feeling grumpy at having been distracted from poking his brother in the eye with a fork by this meaningless drivel.

"But you're missing the point!" fumed Archie impatiently. "This is our chance to assume control of the kingdom."

"How's that?" snuffled Percy drowsily, his snout covered in the scrambled eggs, porridge, and baked beans he had just been in the process of happily gulping down.

"Don't you see?" replied Archie. "When the representative of the king and queen comes to our house to extend an invitation to the palace, it will give us the opportunity we have been seeking for so long."

"You mean…," interrupted Charley, bits of gob-soaked food once again spraying out of his mouth.

"That's right," continued Archie (the brightest and also the meanest of the three pigs). "This is our chance to kill the king and queen."

"But how kin we do tha'?" asked Percy (the most stupid and also the nicest of the three pigs) in a very confused voice. "They're not comin' to visit us live and in person or nothin' like that are they?"

"No, no, dumb head," replied Archie impatiently. "But we can give the representative a small gift to take back to the palace for the king and queen. It's the gift that will kill them."

"Oh, yeah. I see," mumbled Percy, not seeing at all. He stuck his snout back into his scrambled eggs and baked beans, happy to be doing something he understood.

Charley jumped in eagerly at this point. "Brilliant! Absolutely brilliant, Archie! And, I say, there is no time like the present to get to work!"

Archie and Charley leapt up from the table and headed into the back room to devise a plan to kill the king and queen, leaving Percy to his eggs and beans.

After much plotting, scheming, grunting, and snorting, Archie and Charley came up with a wonderful, dastardly, deadly idea. They would build a small bomb that could be placed on a silver platter with a silver domed cover (called a "cloche") to conceal it. They would present this deadly contraption, along with a card made out to the king and queen, to the royal family's representative when he arrived on their doorstep.

"And," giggled Archie excitedly, "when they lift the cloche to see what delightful gift lies in wait for them ... KABOOM! They and all of their followers will be blown to bits."

"Giving us a chance," continued Charley eagerly, "to move in and assume control of the kingdom."

At this precise moment, Percy waddled in on them, eggs, beans, and porridge still coating his snout. "What are yous guys doin?" he asked dozily.

"Plotting our overthrow of the kingdom, dear brother," snorted Archie gleefully.

"Why'd ya wanna do that?" questioned Percy confusedly, having completely forgotten their last conversation.

"So we can assume power and control for ourselves, of course, you imbecile," spat out Archie impatiently.

"But what will the king and queen do if they can't be the king and queen anymore or nothin'?" grunted Percy, more confused than ever.

"They'll be dead, so they won't be doing anything," laughed Charley wickedly.

"Dead?" asked Percy. "Are we goin' to kill 'em then?" (I told you he forgot.)

"Absolutely," answered Archie. "That's the plan."

"But why would we wanna do that? They're really nice and everythin' like that, always helping everyone and givin' out free food and stuff." The distribution of food, naturally, was Percy's primary definition of "nice and everything."

"Don't be stupid," growled Archie nastily. "They're anything but nice. They're keeping us from our rightful position of power and supreme command, after all. What could be crueler than that?"

"Ummmm, I guess thas kind of a good point," mumbled Percy apologetically. He had no idea what they were on about, but didn't want to seem stubborn or argumentative. His brothers could get pretty mad at him at times; and when they were mad, they were mean. After all, if they thought a fork in the eye was amusing, you can only imagine what they would do when they were in a foul mood.

"Okay, then," went on Archie. "Now that we're all on side...." He glared at Percy threateningly, "Why don't we get started? Charley and I will build the bomb and you, Percy, can test it." This only made sense, as Percy was the least important of the pigs as far as Archie was concerned ... and, he certainly couldn't be trusted with bomb building. He was far too stupid for that.

So, Percy happily went back into the kitchen to fix his next meal, leaving Archie and Charley to build themselves a bomb.

Now, it is important to point out here, dear reader, that the king and queen were indeed very nice, in spite of what Archie and Charley had told Percy. Not only did they give out food to all of the citizens of their kingdom who were in need, they also made sure that everyone was treated fairly, equally, and with respect. They showed compassion for every living creature and saw to it that everyone had a roof over their head and the opportunity to learn, grow, and pursue their dreams. The royal family was descended from a long line of beautiful, sleek horses, and they were protected by a pack of loyal wolves who made it their job to see that no harm would ever come to their much beloved king and queen.

It was one of these wolves, by the name of Septuagint, who was destined to call upon the three little pigs in their straw house to invite them to the palace in order to pay their respects to the king and queen. But, strange events were about to unfold that would delay his delivery of the invitation.

Which brings us back to Charley and Archie and their bomb-building project. While Percy had been happily eating his way through every scrap of food in the kitchen, his brothers had been busily preparing a test device.

This device was sitting before them on their work table: a silver platter with a silver domed cloche to conceal the dynamite that lay hidden within its innocent-looking depths.

"We must put it to the test," snorted Charley excitedly. "Before we build the real thing."

"Absolutely," agreed Archie. "There is hardly enough dynamite in this bomb to blow a hole in our work table, never mind blow apart an enormous castle with hundreds of people in it. But it should be sufficient for testing purposes."

Then he called out, "Oh, Percy, dear brother, could you please come here for a minute?"

When Percy trotted in to his brothers' work room, he looked dazedly from one of them to the other.

"Yous want somethin?" he asked, bits of gruel and maple syrup dripping from his snout.

"Yes, dear Percy, indeed we do," replied Archie in a deceptively kind voice. "We need you to test something for us."

"Ah, sure!" grunted Percy, happy to be of service. "Wadaya want I should do?"

"Just lift the silver cloche, would you?" asked Archie sweetly.

"Wha … whas a cloche? Where? What? Huh?" mumbled Percy, looking around, confusion wrinkling his sticky snout.

"The silver cover … on this platter … on the work table," answered Archie, impatiently pointing at the silver cloche that was sitting right in front of Percy's greasy snout.

"Ah, sure," snorted Percy, pleased that he now understood. He went to lift the cover from the platter.

"AH, AH, AH!" yelled out Archie. "Just wait for Charley and me to leave the room." They didn't want to be close by to the device should the explosion be a bit more powerful—and more deadly—than they had planned.

"Sure thin'," replied Percy, completely ignorant of what he was testing, and not much caring. If it wasn't food, he wasn't really interested.

Charley and Archie dashed into the next room, and Percy reached for the cover once more.

KABOOOOOOOOOOOOOOOOOOOOOOOOOOOM!

A tremendous explosion ripped through the house of straw, knocking it to the ground.

A few minutes later, Charley and Archie dragged themselves from the wreckage of their straw house.

"Hmmmm, perhaps we put a touch too much dynamite in it for testing purposes," mused Charley, as he pulled bits of straw off of his sailor suit. "But at least we know it most likely works."

"Good work, Percy," called out Archie, as Percy crawled dazedly from the ruins of the house, the cloche still clutched in one of his trotters, his face covered in soot and bits of burnt straw, as well as a few remaining blobs of gruel. "Now, would you mind building us a new house, Percy, old boy?"

A few days later, Archie, Percy, and Charley were once again seated around their kitchen table gobbling up a light breakfast of pancakes, waffles, maple syrup, pizza, sausages (beef, of course—no pork allowed in the pigs' house), porridge, peas, potato salad, and macaroni and cheese. This time, the house they were sitting in was built out of old twigs and sticks and other bits of rubbish that Percy had been able to pick up without having to go to too much effort. The wind whistled through all of the gaps in the walls because Percy was about as good a house builder as he was a bomb tester, but Archie and Charley didn't care. Soon they would be living in the king and queen's magnificent palace. The house of sticks would be but a distant, drafty memory. Of course, how they planned to live in the castle after they had blown it to bits remained to be seen. But perhaps, not being the smartest of pigs themselves, they hadn't quite gotten around to thinking about this.

"We must get to work building another bomb," said Archie. "I heard that the wolf came by to visit us at our last place after Percy blew it to bits. He obviously couldn't leave our invitation on the pile of smoldering straw. It would have been burnt to a crisp. But it won't be long before he's back knocking at our door once he hears that we've moved into a new home. We must be ready for him when he arrives."

"Gotcha," grinned Charley evilly. "Should we get to work then?"

"We must," snorted Archie, rubbing his trotters together as he thought of all of the gold and silver that would soon be his once the king and queen had exploded. "Not a second to waste. Oh, Percy, dear chap," he said, slapping his brother on the back, causing Percy to choke on the enormous sausage that he had just tried to swallow whole. Archie wrinkled his nose in disgust at his brother's unseemly behavior. "Percy. Stop that. Stop that. RIGHT NOW!" Archie punched Percy in the stomach to try to get him to stop making such annoying choking sounds and the sausage shot out of Percy's mouth hitting Archie squarely in the eye.

"Why you," said Archie furiously raising his trotter to slap Percy again. But then he thought better of it. He wiped his eye and flashed a hateful, insincere smile at Percy who was too busy eyeing the potato salad to notice. "Just make sure nobody bothers Charley or me, old chap," Archie spat out through gritted teeth. "We've got work to do."

He kicked Charley in the backside to encourage him to get a move on; and then, as Charley landed with a loud thud in the next room, he trotted after him.

"Quickly," he hissed at Charley. "We must get the bomb built before the wolf gets here."

"Gotcha," grinned his brother, rubbing his sore behind. "I'm on it." Even with a swollen, aching bottom, he was hardly able to contain his excitement at the thought of moving into the royal palace and having loads of servants to order about and do his every bidding. Of course, he was forgetting, once again, that there would be no servants left if he and Archie carried out their dastardly plot of blowing up the palace and everyone in it. That's what comes from being an evil, stupid pig.

Archie and Charley worked feverishly all through the night and, by morning, they had another bomb ready for Percy to test. They placed it carefully on another silver platter, hiding it beneath another silver domed cloche, and then carried it gingerly out to the main room. They placed it on the table in front of Percy who was either eating today's breakfast or finishing last night's dinner, snorting and snuffling his way through piles of baked beans, tuna casseroles, and cheese omelets.

"Percy, dear boy," said Archie sweetly, "we've brought you a special treat."

Percy looked up at Archie in surprise, his face covered in squashed baked beans and bits of tuna and egg. "Yer what?" he snuffled dopily.

"We've brought you a treat," smiled Archie fakely, honey, sugar, and molasses dripping from his insincere voice.

Percy looked around curiously, wondering where the treat might be hiding.

"There, under that silver cover," said Archie pointing at the silver cloche under which the test bomb had been hidden.

Percy clapped his trotters in happiness and went to lift the lid.

"No, no, wait!" shrieked out Archie. "Charley and I must leave the room first or, or, or it won't be a surprise."

"Oh … right yous are," said Percy sheepishly. "Sorry, Archie, I'm so dumb sometimes."

He waited until Archie and Charley had trotted out of the house as fast as their little, fat pig legs would carry them. Then, eager to find out what wonderful treat was in store for him and wishing as hard as he could that it might be a chocolate cake with butterscotch sauce, he lifted the lid.

KABOOOOOOOOOOOOOOOOOOOOOOOOOOM!

Down went the house of sticks with an ear-splitting clatter as the test bomb blew the whole place to smithereens.

"Well, Percy's gone and done it again," sighed Archie feeling extremely annoyed. "I guess it's back to the drawing board for us, old chap," he sighed self-pityingly, patting Charley on the back.

"Look!" snorted Charley anxiously in reply. "Look there!" He pointed at a figure that was moving swiftly towards the pile of sticks that had once been their house. "Isn't that...?"

"IT IS!" shrieked Archie. "It's the wolf. Quick, let's scarper before he has a chance to deliver that invitation."

They darted into the forest that lay behind their house so they could find a good place to hide.

Huffing and puffing with the effort of running a good ten yards on his porky little legs, Archie panted out, "I just hope that idiot Percy doesn't make a sudden appearance and accept the invitation from that toffy-nosed git of a wolf. All of our wonderful plans will be ruined."

They stared worriedly at their former house from their hiding place behind a tree. They could hear the wolf shouting, "Hallo! Hallo in there! Is everyone all right? Do you need assistance?" But there was no sound.

"Hmmmm," snuffled Archie, "perhaps Percy has kicked the old bucket."

Charley gulped anxiously knowing that, if Percy was gone, he would be the one who would have to build the next house ... and test the next bomb. But he needn't have worried because, only ten hours later, long after the wolf had gone and it was almost dark, a very dazed Percy emerged from the pile of smoldering sticks, carrying a very crispy looking sausage and a trotter-full of burnt-up casserole. He wobbled about, looking up, down, and all around, as if he didn't know where he was, stopping only to take a bite of the sausage or to gulp down a bit of casserole every few seconds and to let out a loud burp.

Finally, Archie, who was snoring peacefully in his hiding place behind the tree, was awakened by all of the chewing, grunting, and belching noises that were going on just a few feet from his head. He peered out from behind the tree and spotted Percy teetering about outside the wreckage of their home. He poked Charley in the eye to wake him up and then roared at Percy who jumped twelve feet in the air because he was so startled. "Well, so there you are, Percival. Finally. Well, you've made a fine mess again, I must say."

Percy started to mumble out, "Sorry, Archie. Didn't mean to be a bumblin' buffoony bozo like I can be. Sorry. It sorta jus' went...." He raised his trotters in the air to demonstrate a bomb exploding and sent bits of casserole and what was left of his sausage flying in all directions.

"Yes, well," said Archie, ducking out of the way of a flying piece of tuna, "all's forgiven. Just get to work building us another house."

"Yessir," snuffled Percy saluting. He started to trot off towards who knows where, picking up bits of sausage and casserole along the way.

"Make it out of something less-blow-upable this time," shouted out Archie.

Percy turned around and started trotting in the opposite direction towards who-knows-where else.

"Make it snappy," roared Archie. "And make sure you get us more bomb-making ... I mean, special inventing pieces, while you're at it," he added.

Percy started charging around in frenzied, confused circles and then, without a moment's notice, he shot off down the road; so fast that he could almost have broken the four-hour mile record for pigs.

It was days later that Percy finally came back, covered in plaster and bits of spaghetti. He found his brothers lounging around the pile of still-smoking sticks, toasting marshmallows.

He smacked his lips hungrily and then blurted out, "House is ready for yers. Wanna come and see?"

"Can't you see we're busy here?" snarled Archie. But he put down his marshmallow and signaled to Charley to get up. "Come on then. I guess we should take a look at what kind of a hovel our stupid brother has gone and built for us this time."

They followed Percy down the road a ways until they came upon a brick house. At least, they assumed it must be a house because it had a door and windows and a roof. Other than that, it just looked like a pile of bricks that had been thrown together any which way. The walls looked as if they would fall over with the least breath of wind, with bricks stuck in all higgledy-piggledy, sideways and upside down and backwards and inside out. Bits of plaster dripped in huge, gloppy lumps down the sides of the house, making it look like a lopsided cake that had far too much icing.

Charley and Archie gaped at the house in dismay. This was by far the worst house that Percy had ever built. One rain shower and they would all be squashed like pancakes when the thing came tumbling down on their heads.

"Why, why, you stupid…," choked out Archie, his pink pig face turning a bright shade of red.

"Perhaps the plaster will hold it together?" said Charley quickly. He was worried that Archie might strangle Percy and then he would be stuck with testing the bomb. No way did he want that to happen.

Archie clenched his teeth and then, remembering that they would have to work quickly if they were going to have another bomb ready when the wolf returned, he hissed, "Okay, okay. Let's get in there and get to work."

Percy held the front door open proudly for his brothers, and Archie and Charley trotted quickly into the house, looking around. The dining room table, which was of course always in the very center of the front room, being the most important spot in the house besides the kitchen, was already piled high with half-eaten apples, mounds of spaghetti, and leftover ends from loaves of bread.

"No time to eat," snapped Archie as Charley made a beeline for the food. "We've got to get to work."

Charley sighed, almost wishing he was Percy after all. Percy got to sit at the table and stuff himself until he was ready to burst. It wasn't fair. He had to do all of the hard work while all Percy had to do was test a silly little bomb or two. Truly not fair at all. Sighing loudly again and casting an evil, jealous, beady-eyed pig look at Percy, he waddled reluctantly after Archie into the next room where Percy had dutifully stored their bomb-making materials.

"We must get it right this time," snuffled Archie. "I'm fed up with living in these poor excuses for houses that our half-wit brother Percy keeps building for us. Mark my words, Charley old chap, I'm going to be in that castle before this week is out."

"I'm with you," snorted Charley, excited once again at the idea of living in the palace. He raised his trotters in what would have been a thumbs-up gesture, if he'd had any thumbs.

"And, clearly," Archie went on, scratching his whiskery chin thoughtfully with one of his trotters, "the bombs all work just fine. No need to test any more of them, really. So why don't we make this one extra powerful and just have it ready for the snotty, stuck-up old wolf when he gets here."

"Yes, yes," grunted Charley eagerly. "Good idea, old man." His mouth watered at the thought of all of the wonderful meals that his servants would make for him once they moved into the palace.

They set to work and, before night had fallen, they had the real bomb ready to go, sitting under yet another silver domed cloche on yet another silver platter. Archie scrawled out a note that read, "To the king and queen with our compliments," and tied it to the handle of the cloche with a piece of ribbon. He then motioned for Charley to follow him.

Trotting out wearily to the main room of the house, they found Percy in his customary spot at the dining room table, his snout buried in peanut butter and jelly, french fries, and chocolate pudding.

"Oh, Percy," warbled Archie in his fake, sweet voice.

Percy looked up, two globs of peanut butter stuck in his nostrils. "Yous wanted me Archie?" he grunted, his mouth full of chewed up french fries. Then, suddenly, he spotted the silver platter and cloche that Charley was holding.

Now, while Percy wasn't the smartest pig on the planet, he also wasn't the stupidest. He wasn't having anything to do with any more silver cloches that went KABOOM whenever you lifted them up.

He squealed in terror, bits of half-digested food flying out of his mouth. He charged out of the house, pushing Archie and Charley out of the way in his haste and sending the silver platter and bomb sailing through the air.

"Quick, don't let it hit the ground!" shouted Archie. "Catch it, you id…"

But it was too late.

The bomb went off with the loudest KABOOM yet.

And, amazingly, it turned out that Charley was quite right about what he'd said earlier… While the blast from the bomb blew the door and the roof off of the brick house, the big globs of plaster on the outside walls did indeed hold the rest of the house together.

When the wolf arrived a couple of hours later, invitation in hand, he found Percy sitting on the front step, snuffling, sniffing, and blowing his snout in a handkerchief that appeared to be covered in blobs of peanut butter.

"What's the matter, dear boy?" said the wolf kindly.

"I don' know where my brothers are," mumbled Percy. "An' all of my dinner got blowed up."

The wolf peered past Percy into the dark main room of the brick house. It was indeed a terrible mess, with bits of exploded furniture and french fries lying about here, there, and everywhere, as well as peanut butter and jelly and chocolate pudding dripping from the walls. However, the pigs had a reputation for being rather messy so he thought nothing of it. He bellowed, "Hallo! Hallo! Anybody home?" into the room, but he got no answer.

Percy started sniffling and blowing his snout loudly again so the wolf walked gingerly into the house. The place was clearly deserted.

But, there, amidst all of the bits of wood and chocolate pudding and blown-apart french fries, there was something that looked a bit out of place. The wolf picked it up carefully and took it outside to get a better look at it.

Percy squealed in horror when he saw the wolf towering above him holding the silver platter and silver cloche, and he took off like a chubby little rocket down the road.

The wolf looked after him in surprise and then looked back at the silver platter and cloche in his paws. Tied to the cloche was a singed note on which he could barely make out the message that Archie had scrawled: "To the king and queen with our compliments."

"How generous," murmured the wolf to himself. "The royal family will be so moved by this thoughtful gesture. I'm sure that it's a delightful gift, but I must just take a peek to make sure that it truly is safe to give it to them."

With that, he lifted the cloche…

And…

Lo and behold!

There on the silver platter lay a mountainous pile of plump, steaming pork sausages.

"It seems a strange gift for pigs to give, but I am sure the king and queen will enjoy them tremendously."

With that, he covered the sausages back up with the cloche and set off for the castle. Just as he had predicted, the king and queen were moved by the thoughtfulness and generosity of the pigs, and thoroughly enjoyed the sausages … although they did wonder at the bits of sailor suit that were scattered here and there amongst them.

In fact, the king and queen enjoyed the sausages so much and were so touched by the pigs' kindness that they declared pork sausages to be the official dish of Liberatus, and even had the image of a sausage embroidered into the nation's flag. They went on to rule the nation under that wonderful sausage flag for many, many more years and were loved by all.

As for the three little pigs, themselves…

When the royal family heard that Archie and Charley seemed to have disappeared for good, they invited sweet, stupid Percy to come and live with them, where he was given a sumptuous apartment with gilt walls and a huge canopied bed. He had servants to tend to his every want and need, and spent his days happily eating royal jellies, fresh bread, roasted pheasants, cream-filled éclairs, baked potatoes with mounds of sour cream, buttery shortbread cookies, chocolate cake with butterscotch sauce, and, well, anything his heart—and his stomach—desired. Although, he never did develop a taste for pork sausages. All in all, Percy was a very happy pig and, when he wasn't eating, he was fond of telling people that all of his very best wishes had come true, and could he please have a little more butterscotch sauce for his chocolate cake, thank you.

Of course, Archie's and Charley's most heartfelt wish had also come true. They did end up in the castle after all. They just didn't expect that it would be on the king's plate.

The End

Try to rule the world with hate,
and you'll end up on someone's plate.

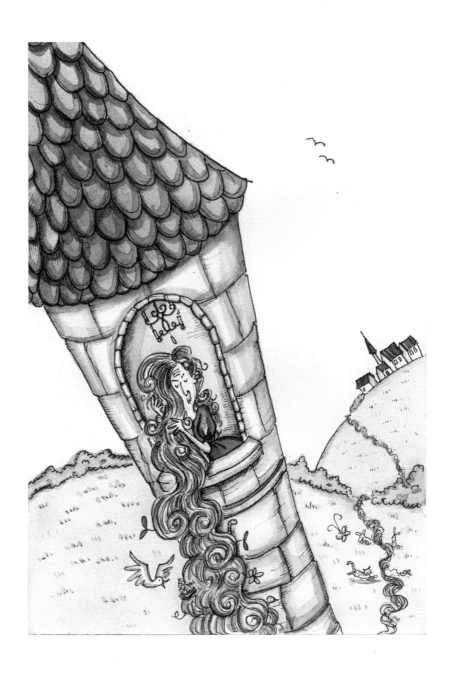

Rapunzel

Once upon a time in a land far, far away there lived a man and woman who had no children, which of course was not an unusual thing in the least.

Then, one fine spring day, the woman discovered that she was going to have a baby, which, if truth be told, was also not particularly strange.

But here's where things *do* get very, very odd.

Rather than craving sweets or pickles or pigs' feet, as most women do when they are expecting a child, this woman wanted nothing but salad. She wished for salad at breakfast, salad at lunch, salad at dinner, salad for her in-between-time snacks, and salad for every other minute of the day. She would even get up in the middle of the night to munch on a head of lettuce and a stack of tomatoes.

It is no wonder, then, that when her baby girl was finally born there was something not quite right about her. To begin with, this not-quite-rightness was barely noticeable … just the odd green sprout here and there on her little, bald baby head.

But, as she grew older, the sprouts grew and grew until, lo and behold, they turned into large green lettuce leaves which, you will have to admit, was very peculiar, very peculiar indeed.

It was because of this odd hairdo that the little girl's parents decided to bless their daughter with the charming, exceedingly appropriate name Rapunzel. Now, you might be thinking, what does the name Rapunzel have to do with green, leafy hair? Well, quite a bit actually. You see, Rapunzel is just another word for lettuce.

So there you have it.

I don't think I need tell you that Rapunzel wasn't very fond of her name (would you like to be called "lettuce" or "onion" or "carrot," after all?), and she really, really, especially hated her unusual head covering. It brought her no end of misery. The cook was always asking if she could tear a leaf or two off to use in the salad she was making for lunch. Her lettuce-loving mother could never resist having a little taste when she leaned over to kiss her daughter at night. And Rapunzel couldn't even dream of sunbathing in the sumptuous garden of her parents' magnificent castle without rabbits hopping up to nibble hungrily at her head. This annoyed her so much that every once in a while Rapunzel would make a grab for one of the bunnies, hoping that Cook would turn it into a delicious rabbit stew, and teach it what it felt like to be gnawed upon for a change, but she was never quick enough to catch the fleet-footed animals.

As the days and months wore on and her head became leafier and leafier, Rapunzel grew grumpier and meaner and madder. She hated everyone who didn't resemble a vegetable like her … which meant, of course, that she hated absolutely everybody, with the exception of Elsie, the head maid, who had a face like a tomato (which is technically a fruit, but looks similar enough to a vegetable to be considered acceptable in Rapunzel's eyes).

"I hate you!" she would scream at her parents, especially if they happened to be eating a salad at the time.

"I hate you!" she yelled at the butler and cook and stable hand.

"I hate you!" she shouted at the birds and bees that flitted around the walls of her beautiful home.

"I hate you!" she screeched at the rabbits who hopped around her, giggling in their annoying bunny way, as she tried to snatch them up.

"And I ESPECIALLY hate you!" she shrieked at her cousin, Flavia, who lived with Rapunzel and her parents because her own parents were dead, as they so often were in olden times. It was easy to see why Rapunzel would hate her cousin so much. Flavia had infuriatingly lovely lavender eyes, detestably soft pink cheeks, a gruesomely sweet smile, and, worst of all, horrifyingly beautiful golden curls that fell almost to her waist. Rapunzel longed to rip those curls right off of Flavia's head. She would tug at them whenever Flavia gave her a loving, cousinly hug, hoping beyond hope that her golden locks would detach themselves from her scalp. But they never did. And no matter how much Rapunzel made Flavia's head ache with all of the hair-pulling she did, Flavia kept right on trying to cheer up the miserable, grouchy Rapunzel by hugging her every chance that she got. Flavia hated to see anyone unhappy. But Flavia's efforts to raise the spirits of her cousin met with no more success than Rapunzel's attempts to render Flavia bald.

In fact, the more Flavia tried to make Rapunzel feel better, the angrier and more hateful Rapunzel became. "How dare she mock me the way that she does?" she growled, kicking little mice out of the way as she stomped and stamped through her garden. "Who does she think she is always showing off that despicable hairdo of hers?" she snarled, ripping the petals off of every flower she passed. "What a horrible little...," she started to grumble, but before she could finish her sentence, she stopped short. There, on the branch of a rose bush, sat a fabulously beautiful golden-winged butterfly.

"Why, that nasty bug just reminds me of hideous old Flavia with her ridiculous yellow curls," fumed Rapunzel. "I'll teach it to be so mean and gloating. Try to shame me with your golden-ness, would you?" She made a grab for the butterfly and tugged at its wings, huffing and puffing and grunting as she tried to tear them off.

Suddenly, a small squeal came out of the butterfly's mouth, which meant, of course, that the butterfly wasn't really a butterfly at all, but was—as you have probably already guessed—a little fairy. "Please don't hurt me," begged the fairy, in her most pleading, terrified voice.

"Why shouldn't I?" snapped Rapunzel, who was just as happy to rip the golden wings off a fairy as off a butterfly. "I hate you."

"But why should you hate me?" trembled the fairy. "You don't even know me!"

"I hate you because of your stupid yellow wings. They mock me," growled Rapunzel.

"I don't mean them to," pleaded the fairy. "I was just born this way."

"Well, too bad for you then," snapped Rapunzel and she tugged at the fairy's wings again.

"Please, please don't," begged the fairy.

"Give me one good reason why I shouldn't," snarled Rapunzel.

"Because," replied the fairy, with a quiver in her voice, "it wouldn't be a very nice thing to do?"

Rapunzel laughed. "Ha, ha, ha! What do I care about being nice?" and she pulled even harder on the fairy's wings.

"Because, because," stammered the fairy quickly, "it wouldn't be the right thing for a little girl to do. Little girls are so sweet and kind."

"I'm not," scowled Rapunzel, which was, of course, the truth.

"Um, um," began the fairy, racking her little brain for a reason that would work with such a nasty, jealous creature. "Because," she said finally, keeping her fairy fingers crossed, "because I will grant you your fondest wish if you let me go."

Rapunzel's eyes lit up with delight. "My fondest wish, you say?" she whispered softly.

The little fairy nodded.

"Well, that's simple," smiled Rapunzel greedily. "I wish for lustrous hair that will grow longer than anyone else's in the whole world … and especially than Flavia's. I want it to grow more and more every day … and, oh yes, I want it to be golden, far, far more goldishly golden than horrible Flavia's."

The fairy, who was very kindhearted, even when having her wings pulled, was worried that having hair that grew more and more all the time might turn out to be more of a curse than a blessing for Rapunzel, so she asked carefully, trying not to anger the girl, "Are you sure that you want this wish? Wouldn't you rather wish for happiness or love or friendship or some wonderful talent that would allow you to do good in the world?"

"No! Of course not!" snapped Rapunzel. "What a stupid wish that would be! Now give me my long golden hair or I will rip off your wings and eat them for lunch."

The fairy shivered at the thought and then sighed sadly at what she was about to do. "Your wish is my command," she whispered, and then she blinked three times, wiggled her nose, patted her head, and stuck her finger in her ear.

As soon as she did this, the lettuce leaves dropped off Rapunzel's head and lush, golden hair started to sprout in their place.

Even though Rapunzel hadn't really planned to let the fairy go once her wish had been granted—because how great would it be, after all, to have wishes granted every day?—she was so thrilled by what was happening on her head that she dropped the fairy so that she could run her fingers through her wonderful, new, better-than-Flavia's, goldishly golden curls.

"I will be beautiful now," smirked Rapunzel. "More beautiful than anyone who has ever lived. Now everyone will have to do as I say ... or I won't let them so much as look at gorgeous me."

As soon as this thought popped into her head, she knew that she had to find a mirror so she could gaze upon her new-found loveliness. She ran home as quickly as her legs would carry her, tripping on her hair every few feet, as it was growing so fast it was now down past her ankles. "Flavia could never grow hair as long as mine!" she laughed happily.

When she got to the front door of her house, she pushed past the family's butler who had opened the door for her and ran up the stairs to her bedroom, ignoring the surprised gasps of her parents and Flavia who, quite understandably, didn't recognize the strange hairy person who was charging towards Rapunzel's room.

"Quick! Quick! After her!" screamed Rapunzel's mother, the Duchess of Zwiebel. "She is a murderer determined to kill my beloved daughter!"

The butler, who had just managed to get back to his feet after being knocked down by Rapunzel, did his best impersonation of a statue and moved not one single muscle. The idea of the nasty Rapunzel being murdered sounded quite nice to him. He wasn't about to dash off to stop it from happening. Certainly not. Life would be so pleasant without her around.

"Oh, heaven help us! Get after her, man!" roared Rapunzel's father, the Duke of Zwiebel, at the butler. While the duke didn't really care for the idea of his only daughter being killed, he, quite naturally, didn't want to face a murderer himself, so he wasn't about to go anywhere near that hairy, golden crazy person. That's what servants were for, after all … to be killed instead of him.

The butler still refused to budge and both of Rapunzel's parents now lay fainting with fright on the floor, so Flavia sprinted up the stairs to save her cousin.

When she got to Rapunzel's room, she peeked through the doorway. Her knees trembled with fear and her heart pounded in her chest. "Oh, what will I do if there really is a murderer in Rapunzel's bedroom?" she thought to herself, terror gripping her soul. She gave herself a shake to try to make herself feel a bit more courageous. Which it didn't, of course. Shaking never does do anything besides make your brain rattle around in your skull. So, still feeling absolutely terrified, as well she should, Flavia gritted her teeth and mumbled as bravely as she could, "I'll do what I must to save poor Rapunzel." Then, she stormed into Rapunzel's room, the fiercest look she could muster plastered across her charming, sweet, unferocious, completely unscary face.

"Oh my goodness!" she shrieked, feeling as if she might faint as dead away as the Duke and Duchess of Zwiebel. "What is that hideous creature that I see before me?" There, in front of Rapunzel's bedroom mirror, sat what looked to be a large yellow fur ball.

"Don't be so jealous," chortled Rapunzel, more good-naturedly than she had chortled anything for a long time. "Hideous, indeed! What a thing to say! Have you ever seen such a glorious head of hair?"

As soon as Rapunzel uttered these words, Flavia realized that the fur ball sitting in front of the mirror was not a fur ball at all but was, in fact, her cousin. She tumbled to the ground in the faint that she had thought she was going to have mere moments before, but didn't, until just now that is. Very confusing. The point is … she fainted.

Two days later, when she finally regained consciousness, Flavia saw that her cousin was still sitting in front of the mirror, gazing at her reflection. Rapunzel's hair had grown even longer since Flavia had fainted. Her curls now flowed almost to the door.

Flavia untangled herself from the long tendrils of hair that had wound themselves around her while she lay on the floor, and, still feeling a bit wobbly, she staggered to her feet. "What happened to you, dear cousin?" stuttered Flavia, staring at the mounds of hair sprouting from her cousin's once leafy scalp.

"My fondest wish came true, of course," smiled Rapunzel smugly. "And now I am far more beautiful than you. Not that you were ever beautiful of course," she added quickly.

Flavia started to walk towards Rapunzel so that she could get a better look at her cousin, but Rapunzel screamed at her, "Get off my hair, you clumsy, big-footed oaf! You'll give me split ends! Get out of my room, and never come back!"

Flavia tiptoed out of the room as quickly as she could, trying not to trample her cousin's hair overly much.

"Some people!" muttered Rapunzel as she turned back to the mirror to stare at herself once more. "So envious of another person's gorgeousness."

Flavia raced down the stairs where she found Rapunzel's parents having afternoon tea in the dining room. They happily munched away on scones with fresh strawberry jam and clotted cream while Flavia tried to catch her breath and steady her nerves.

She knew she must tell them what had befallen their daughter, but hardly knew where to begin.

"Have some tea and scones, dear," smiled Rapunzel's mother, breaking into Flavia's thoughts. "You look worn out. Did you get rid of the murderer?"

Flavia nodded, not sure whether or not nodding was exactly the correct response.

"Jolly good," muttered Rapunzel's father with his mouth full of pastries, jam, and cream. "Now help yourself to some scones, what? Pip, pip." He took another bite of a scone himself.

"I, I…," stuttered Flavia, too shocked and concerned to eat. "Rapunzel … her hair.…"

"Yes, it is a shame about that," sighed Rapunzel's mother. "I think perhaps I shouldn't have eaten quite so much salad while I was pregnant with her. Green is such a difficult color. It does tend to clash so."

"Quite right, dear," chortled Rapunzel's father as he bit into his tenth scone.

"But her hair," panted Flavia. "It's changed. It's goldishly golden and long and…"

"Well, she'll certainly be pleased about that," interrupted Rapunzel's mother. "She must be terribly hungry. Growing hair is very demanding work … and she hasn't eaten for two days. Bring her down for a spot of tea, won't you, Charles?" she asked, turning to the butler, who, while sorry that Rapunzel hadn't been murdered, was hoping that having a new hairdo would make her a little less grumpy.

He was wrong of course.

He hadn't even entered Rapunzel's room when her angry screams could be heard throughout the castle and into the surrounding village. "Get off my hair, you big brute of an idiot! You are ruining my hairstyle!"

It seems that the butler had carelessly trodden upon one of Rapunzel's curls, which had now slithered their way out her bedroom door and into the hallway. He quickly turned around and charged down the stairs. "And tell no one to bother me," Rapunzel yelled after him. "I don't want any more clumsy people stomping all over my beautiful tresses, you stupid fool."

The butler reappeared in the doorway to the dining room, as red in the face as the maid whose head, as you will recall, resembled a tomato. "She says…"

"We heard," sighed Rapunzel's mother. She got up from the dining room table very reluctantly. She was sure that, as soon as she turned her back, her greedy-guts of a husband would polish off all that remained of the scones. She had eaten only eleven so far and planned on gulping down at least twenty more before dinner. She cast him a threatening look to let him know that she would punish him severely should he gobble up every last one of the pastries, but he was far too busy stuffing the wonderful confections into his mouth to notice. Sighing again, she wandered over to the foot of the staircase that led to the floor above. "Rapunzel," she yelled up the stairs, angry that her daughter was depriving her of her favorite afternoon snack. "Rapunzel, I know you must be absolutely starving. Come down for tea, right this minute."

"NO!" shouted Rapunzel, who didn't want to leave her mirror.

"Should we bring something up?" asked her mother, looking anxiously over her shoulder at her husband, who was quickly making his way through the mound of scones on the dining room table. She was eager to bring this conversation to an end.

"NO!" screeched Rapunzel, who didn't want anyone tromping on her hair.

"Well, how will you eat then?"

Rapunzel thought for a moment. "I'll lower a basket from my bedroom window and you can put my meals in that," she said. "And you're not to come up here … ever."

"But how will we go to bed if we're not allowed upstairs?" asked her mother. "Our bedrooms are on the second floor just as yours is."

"Too bad for you," shrieked Rapunzel. "You'll just have to make do down there. Stop bothering me and get me some scones and tea."

Rapunzel looked around her bedroom to see what she could use as a basket and what she could use to lower whatever the basket might be out of the window. Now, some versions of Rapunzel's famous story would have you believe that she used her hair for tasks such as this, but don't believe any of them. Not a single one. Rapunzel knew that pulling things up and down with her long, flowing curls would give her the most terrible case of split ends ever known to man, woman, or girl. No way was she going to allow that to happen. No. Instead, she decided to tie together all of the priceless satin sheets from her bed to create two long ropes. These she tied to the handles of her bedpan (which, as you probably know, is a pot into which people used to pee in the days before toilets). "Perfect!" she smiled to herself. "Just the thing to get my food to me."

She lowered the bedpan to the ground outside of her window, and when the butler placed a few scones, some strawberry jam and clotted cream, a pot of tea, a tea cup, plate, and silverware in it, she pulled it up without so much as a thank you or fare thee well.

As she stuffed the scones down her throat (growing hair was ravenous work, after all, just as her mother had said), she mused to herself, "Before long, this room won't be big enough for me and my wonderful hair. My glorious curls are going to get all squashed and knotted and nasty. I must do something to fix this dastardly dilemma. Or, rather, other people must fix it for me because, well, I'm far too gorgeous for that sort of thing now. "

She pondered over her problem for a while and then, clapping her hands together with glee, she shouted, "By Jove, I've got it! Yes, siree, Bob's your uncle and that makes Bob your cousin, too! Hip hip hurray!"

"Mother! Father!" she shouted, hoping that they could hear her wherever they might be.

"Yes, dear," came her mother's voice from the dining room, where she was just finishing off her twenty-fourth scone, the duke having kindly left her a few after all.

"You must get the tower room ready for me this second," yelled back Rapunzel. "I need to move there immediately."

"But why, dear?" asked her mother, her mouth full of clotted cream and strawberry jam.

"Just BECAUSE," snarled Rapunzel. "Just do as I say, or, or...."

Her mother didn't wait to hear what the "or" might be—she had witnessed her daughter's wrath enough times to know better—and quickly shouted back, "Of course, dear. We'll have the servants prepare the oh-so-charming tower room tout de suite so you can move in there this evening."

"That's more like it," grunted Rapunzel. She muttered to herself, "Some people are so thick. Anyone with half a brain would know why I want to move into the tower room without having to ask me to explain myself."

And, because you have far more than half a brain, dear reader, I know that you already know that Rapunzel wanted to move into the tower because it was so tremendously tall. Her long curls could flow out the window of her new bedroom and they wouldn't even touch the ground; it was that tall. Very, very tall. Extraordinarily tall. Almost a skyscraper, in fact.

As the days and months and years passed, Rapunzel's hair continued to grow and she remained shut in the tower, gazing happily at her reflection in the mirror. Her parents eventually died of old age, and Flavia grew into a lovely young woman with a husband and four sweet children of her own. Still Rapunzel didn't leave her room... not to attend her parents' funerals, not to be a bridesmaid at Flavia's wedding, not to visit her cousin's sweet little children, not to eat, not even to go to the bathroom. She had Elsie, the tomato-faced servant, bring all of her meals to her room, which, as you can imagine, was perfectly acceptable now that Rapunzel's hair was hanging out the window and wasn't in danger of being trampled, and she began using her bedpan for peeing in rather than for transporting scones up and down.

Anyone who tried to visit her at the castle was soon chased off. Rapunzel would hurl bits of half-eaten food out her window at them, laughing hysterically each time she managed to hit them square on the top of their heads. She especially loved to throw soup and eggs because they were so wonderfully messy.

Even a handsome, young prince who came to see her one day, hoping that he might win the hand of such a wealthy, young woman, was soon sent packing. When he yelled out, "Rapunzel, Rapunzel, let down your golden hair," she roared back, "It's already hanging out the window, you idiot! Are you a complete and utter numbskull or something?"

The prince, not to be deterred by such lighthearted remarks when he had the chance of becoming so much more fabulously rich than he already was if only Rapunzel would marry him, shouted back in his most charming voice, "Forgive me, fair lady! I was momentarily blinded by your glorious beauty and did not see your golden curls!"

While Rapunzel liked to be called beautiful by someone other than herself, she was furious that he hadn't noticed her wonderful hair.

"Just as I thought … you *are* a numbskull," she screeched. And she threw the contents of her bedpan at him.

Soaked from head to toe and feeling a bit sick, the prince finally got the hint. He jumped back on his white charger and galloped off towards the horizon, never to bother Rapunzel again.

"Good riddance," smirked Rapunzel, turning back to gaze at her reflection once more. "I really *am* beautiful," she sighed happily.

Now, while Rapunzel was clearly brilliant at scaring off most everyone who came to the castle to see her, there was one person who refused to stop visiting her no matter what Rapunzel threw at her. That person, of course, was her cousin Flavia.

Every day, come rain or shine, Flavia would walk twenty miles from her own little cottage to Rapunzel's castle. "Dear, Rapunzel," she would shout from the base of the tower miles and miles below her cousin's window, "please let me bring my children to see you. I would so love you to meet them!"

"Go away!" Rapunzel would shriek from the safety of her room. "I don't want any nasty little children grabbing at my hair with their grubby paws! Go away, I say!"

Saddened by her cousin's response, Flavia would turn around and walk the twenty miles home.

But each day, come hail or snow or tornadoes, she would return to the tower, determined that she could convince Rapunzel to see her children. She was worried that her cousin must be terribly lonely and longed to bring some affection and happiness into her life.

Rapunzel would have none of it. Each day she shouted at Flavia to go away and stay away, throwing bowls of porridge and rotten potatoes out of the window at her to make her point.

Eventually, after many more years had passed, Flavia did stop her visits to the tower. She had become too old and frail to walk the twenty miles to Rapunzel's castle. Instead, she spent all of her days surrounded by her loving family, watching her grandchildren play happily in the garden that surrounded her cottage.

Rapunzel was both pleased and annoyed that Flavia had stopped visiting. Pleased that her hair was no longer in danger of being mussed up, but annoyed that Flavia was too selfish to take the time to drop by. "Some people only think of themselves, it would seem," she sighed self-pityingly. "Does she think it's easy living in a tower room with no one for company but a stupid old fruit-that-looks-like-a-vegetable-faced servant who never does get any of my orders right?"

She sighed again and then glanced at her reflection in the mirror to cheer herself up.

"AAAAAARRRRRRRGGGGGGGGHHHHHHHHHH!" she screamed. "What is that, that thing growing out of my head?"

She looked more closely and saw that a long, crinkly white hair was springing forth from her scalp like an ugly old weed. She plucked it out as quickly as she could, but the very next day when she gazed into the mirror again, she saw not one, but six white hairs sprouting amongst her golden tresses. She ripped them out too, but the next day, ninety-eight white hairs had taken their place. Soon, the white hairs were growing faster than she could tear them out until, finally, there wasn't one golden hair left on her head. She had turned completely white.

"Well, this certainly stinks," she grumbled to herself. "Although … at least my hair is still long and relatively lovely. Something to be said for that."

Hah! Not for long, I'm glad to say.

Just a few months later, her crinkly white hair started falling out in handfuls and then in bucketfuls, and finally in stablefuls. It was only a matter of time before she was completely and utterly bald.

With no hair left for anyone to trample upon, Rapunzel could finally leave the castle, but she had nowhere to go and no one to see. She remained shut in her tower room, a lonely, bald woman. "People are so self-centered," she would grumble to herself, thinking about how mean it was of Flavia to have stopped coming to see her, just when she needed her most, the horrible brute.

And then one day, surprise, surprise, Rapunzel did have a visitor. There, at the foot of the tower, was Flavia's thirteen-year-old granddaughter, Emeline, sitting on a white mare and calling out to her.

"Rapunzel, Rapunzel," shouted Emeline (because, remember, the tower was very tall), "my grandmother, your cousin Flavia, is on her death bed and has asked me to bring you to her so that she can see you one last time."

"What on earth is that terrible noise?" whinged Rapunzel. She pulled herself out of the bed in which she spent all of her time napping, snoring, and complaining now that she didn't feel like gazing at herself in the mirror anymore. She clomped over to the window yelling crossly, "Who is it that awakens me from my beauty sleep – not that I need any – so rudely?"

She stuck her pointy bald head out the window and saw beneath her a pretty young girl with the most beautiful head of copper-colored hair she had ever laid eyes upon. Immediately she was overcome with jealousy. But before she could screech the rude words she wanted to screech at the girl, a wicked plan took root inside her shiny skull. "I'm not feeling too well, I'm afraid, my dear," she croaked in her best fake sick-person voice. "Come back tomorrow and I'll go with you then."

"Thank you, oh thank you, dearest Rapunzel!" shouted Emeline happily. "Seeing you will mean so much to my grandmother! Until tomorrow then!" She dug her heels into the white mare, and both horse and rider galloped back to her grandmother's cottage to deliver the good news.

Of course, Rapunzel had no intention of visiting Flavia's cottage. Heaven forbid! She might encounter more copper-haired beauties there!

Oh, no. She had a much, much better idea.

She changed out of her filthy old nightgown and into a ratty dress that had become quite threadbare and moth bitten after having been left hanging in Rapunzel's closet for so many years. No matter. She was on a mission and clothes were of little importance.

She skittered down the hundreds of stairs that led from her tower room to the ground floor and then bolted out the front door of the castle.

As soon as she found herself outside, her heart began pounding like a mad thing.

"Oh, my goodness me!" she shrieked. "I'm having a heart attack! That cruel, cruel girl has killed me with her visit!" She clutched at her chest preparing to faint dead away in an appropriately melodramatic fashion. But, before she could hit the ground, her heart began beating normally once more.

"Well, well, I never," she muttered. "It must just have been the shock of seeing nothing but that big nasty blue sky above my head that set my heart a-twittering." And, for once, she was quite right. For seventy or so years, she had lived in her cozy tower room with a comforting roof over her. Her poor bald head felt quite exposed in the great outdoors.

But now that she was feeling much more like her cruel, old, healthy self again, she was more determined than ever to set her plan in motion,

Off she went through the still-beautiful gardens of the castle, hunting high and low, peering into each rose bush as eagerly as she had once gazed at herself in the mirror.

"Where are you, you lying, deceitful little fairy?" she called out softly, for—you guessed it—she was hunting for that same little, golden-winged fairy who had once granted her wish for long, lustrous hair. "I've got a bone to pick with you," she muttered through clenched teeth.

After five and a half hours of searching, she finally found what she was looking for. There, in the deepest, darkest depths of one of the rose bushes, she saw the merest glimmer of gold.

She thrust her hand into the bush and snatched out the fairy. The poor little fairy, who had been asleep just a moment ago, shrieked in terror when she saw Rapunzel's face glaring at her.

"You...," the fairy gasped.

"Yes, it's me," snarled Rapunzel. "And just look at my head. I'm bald as an acorn. What do you think of that? How do you think my wish worked out, heh?"

The fairy trembled in Rapunzel's claw of a hand, too frightened to speak.

"I should tear you limb from limb," growled Rapunzel, thinking that this would actually be quite a bit of fun, even if it did ruin her plan. But, luckily for the fairy, Rapunzel suddenly remembered just how brilliant her scheme truly was, and so she said, "You're fortunate that I'm such a good-natured, kind, sweet person. I'm going to let you off easy."

The fairy caught sight of Rapunzel's evil smile and worry creased her tiny brow. What would Rapunzel want in return for her freedom this time? A plague upon the land? Famine? War? A pot of gold? A new dress? "I won't grant any of those wishes if she asks for them," she thought determinedly to herself, "except perhaps for the new dress. That one looks like rubbish." She jumped when Rapunzel's croaky voice cut into her thoughts.

"I want my golden hair back," Rapunzel blurted out. "Only longer this time and stronger, so it never falls out."

The fairy thought back on all of the years she had watched Rapunzel sitting alone in the tower room with nothing but her streaming hair for company. "Are you sure you wouldn't like something else?" she urged quietly. "Like love or happiness ... or a new dress?"

Rapunzel squeezed the fairy tighter and said, "NO! Give me my hair back! It was the best thing that ever happened to me!"

"But it kept you a prisoner in your own home," squeaked the fairy, gasping for breath.

"Hah!" snorted Rapunzel. "Me? A prisoner? That's a laugh, that is! I WANTED to stay in my room, you numbskull; away from all of the stupid, jealous oafs who kept trying to wreck my beautiful hairdo. It was the perfect place to be ... high above the rest of the world, like the glorious angel I am."

"GAG!" choked the fairy.

"What's that you're saying?" growled Rapunzel suspiciously.

"Nothing, nothing," stammered the fairy. "You're just holding me a bit too tight." She then added, seeing that she couldn't possibly talk Rapunzel out of making a second foolish wish, "Let's begin then, shall we? Pat your head five times, then pinch your bottom four times, pick your nose once, and scratch your underarm like a monkey."

Rapunzel did as the fairy asked and... VOILA! Lo and behold! Glorious goldishly golden curls began to stream out of her head like a goldishly golden waterfall.

She let go of the fairy, who flew away as quickly as her battered wings would let her, and then she raced back up the stairs to her tower room. She laughed with glee as she caught sight of herself in her mirror. "It's back! It's back!" she roared excitedly.

She jumped up and down on her bed like a half-crazed schoolgirl and then pulled a chair up to the window of her room to wait for Emeline's return. "Now, just wait until you see me, you useless young girl!" she chuckled to herself. "Your ugly hair is NOTHING compared to mine!"

She sat by the window all night waiting excitedly for her first glimpse of Emeline.

When she spotted the girl riding up to the foot of the tower on her white mare, Rapunzel had to cover her mouth with her hands, she began laughing so hard. "I mustn't let her hear me," she thought to herself, holding her sides to prevent them from splitting (not an easy thing to do when you're also covering your mouth). "I don't want to spoil the lovely surprise!" At that, she gave such a joyous guffaw, she fell off her chair. She quickly climbed back on and readied herself for the annoyingly cheery shout she knew she would soon hear from below.

"Well, that girl won't be cheery for long," Rapunzel chuckled to herself, and, as she was chuckling away with her head full of pleasantly nasty thoughts, she heard Emeline call out, "Dear Rapunzel! I've come to take you to visit my grandmother. She can hardly wait to see you!"

"This is it," sneered Rapunzel, "the moment of glory!" She leaned her head out of the window and let her hair tumble down. It had grown so long, that it now touched the ground miles and miles below.

Emeline's horse backed away in fright, but Emeline could do nothing but stare in shock at the long, flowing curls that seemed ready to smother her and the white mare.

"I can see you're awestruck, as well you should be," smirked Rapunzel. "Now, be off with you, you dirty child. The last thing I need is some grubby lout messing up my beautiful hair ... which is so much prettier than yours, by the way. If you so much as touch one single curl, I will come down there and squash you senseless."

Emeline could tell that Rapunzel meant every terrible word that she said. She dug her heels into her horse and galloped off, trembling with terror, never to return to the castle.

Rapunzel laughed hysterically and fell off her chair again. She lay on the floor kicking her feet in the air with sheer and utter delight at all that had just happened. "Oh, isn't life just so, so perfect, my darling," she chortled, speaking to herself, of course, as she had no other darlings in her life … or anyone at all, in fact, with the exception of her poor, old, faithful, tomato-faced servant.

Now, you might expect that the story would end here, with Rapunzel feeling joyous and glad and living happily ever after. Well, as you know, this is a *true* story, not a made-up fairy tale, which means that there is much more that is yet to be told. Or, at least, there is a little bit more to be told.

You see, as the months passed, Rapunzel got her wish … and then some. Her hair continued to grow longer and longer and it was so strong that not even an axe would have been able to hack through it, if Rapunzel had wanted to chop it off … which she didn't. Eventually, it grew so long that it spread across the whole garden and got tangled up in the rose bushes, flowers, and weeds. It soon lost all of its glorious goldishly golden sheen and became instead a home for slugs, worms, and beetles, all of which loved to crawl up Rapunzel's messy curls to visit her in her lofty tower room.

So, Rapunzel did have company in her old age after all.

And best of all, the mounds of hair that covered the ground served as a wonderful, warm, fluffy home for a certain little fairy … who lived happily ever after, even if Rapunzel absolutely didn't.

The End

If envy makes you a nasty thug,
your only friend will be a slug.

Hansel and Gretel

Long, long ago (proving that fairy tales don't have to begin with "once upon a time")…. Long, long ago all old ladies who had the bad luck to sprout hooked noses and hairy warts were believed to be witches. This is very sad and very wrong, because almost all people grow warts and hooked noses when they get old. You can just imagine then how many supposed witches there once were, mixed in with all of the real ones.

Well, at the time this story took place, a particularly warty, hook-nosed old woman was living in the forest with her favorite and only grandson, Peter. Poor Peter's parents had died, but fortunately for him, his grandmother loved him so much that she was willing to do absolutely anything for him. Nana Myrtle (that being the grandmother's name, of course) didn't have very much money, but she was extremely creative and extraordinarily kind. She wanted her little grandson to have everything his charming, sweet child heart could desire to make up for the pitiful fact that he had to live with an old woman who looked like a wicked witch instead of with a mother and father.

And this is why, even though Nana Myrtle was too poor to buy a regular house in the village with stone walls, a wooden door, and a thatched roof, she set about building Peter something almost as good … or even better, perhaps, depending on whether or not you happen to have a sweet tooth and love cookies, candies, cakes, and such things (and who, besides old Lady Tightwad, doesn't, I ask you?). You see, Nana Myrtle was a wonderful baker. She could bake anything: brownies, cupcakes, pies, gingerbread, anything that was worth eating. And, so, she baked her grandson a lovely, two-bedroom cottage. The little house stood deep in the forest on the edge of town because, naturally, zoning laws wouldn't allow gingerbread houses to be built in the village. This particular law was very important because, if grandmothers started building gingerbread houses all over town, well, soon everyone might want one. Then, all of the stonemasons would find themselves without jobs and would start a revolt, and there would be chaos, disaster, death, and destruction everywhere. Terrible. So, as I said, the house was in the forest.

Every day when Peter woke up and took a bite out of his candy floss bed, he thanked his lucky stars that his grandmother wasn't the sort of cook who preferred to prepare broccoli, Brussels sprouts, spinach, cows' brains, and other nasty, healthy stuff instead of the really good things in life, like candies and cake.

"Hurrah for cookies and gingerbread and cupcakes!" he would cheer. "And hurrah for Nana Myrtle!"

In this way, the grandmother who looked like a witch and the little boy who had no parents were able to live together very happily until—you know it just had to happen—one fateful day when they went skipping merrily (well, at least Peter skipped; the grandmother was far too old and rickety for such behavior, so she just hobbled merrily) off to the lake in the deepest darkest depths of the forest. They were on the hunt for duck eggs, which Nana Myrtle needed in order to bake Peter a special bicycle for his birthday. Nana Myrtle and Peter knew that they would be gone all day because the lake was miles and miles away from the little gingerbread house; so Nana Myrtle, being a practical old woman, packed a large picnic basket filled with chocolate chip cookies, a seven layer butter cream cake, and two dozen butter tarts to take with them. "That should last us 'til dinner," she said, smiling fondly at Peter.

"Hurrah for Nana Myrtle! And hurrah for cookies, butter tarts, and butter cream cake," sang Peter, and off he went skippingly with his hobbling old, kindhearted grandmother in search of eggs.

"Hurrah! Hurrah!"

But now, dear reader, while Peter and Nana Myrtle are off egg hunting, I fear that I must introduce you to two more characters who play a very important role in this heart-wrenching tale. Their names, if you haven't already guessed from the title of this story, were Hansel and Gretel. Hansel and Gretel were the two greediest, most selfish children you could ever hope not to meet. Their parents doted upon them and gave them all that they ever demanded: dolls, cookies, balls, and spinning tops. (There were no video games, computers, and flat-screen televisions in those days, or you can be sure that they would have been given all of those, too.) Hansel and Gretel were always dressed in the finest silks and satins onto which had been sewn hundreds of thousands of diamonds, emeralds, rubies, and other precious gems to make the children look that much more special, spoiled, and rich. But, no matter what they were given, it was never enough. They always wanted more, more, more.

One day at school, while Hansel was shooting spitballs at the teacher, and Gretel was dipping her best friend's braids in the ink well on her little wooden desk, they overheard two other children whispering about a certain old witch who lived with an orphan boy in the forest.

"I heard that they live in a house made out of gingerbread, candies, and cookies," whispered the first child.

"Yes, well, I heard that if you venture near the place, the wicked old witch who lives there will eat you for dinner. She made the house out of gingerbread, candy, and cookies just to trick children into going there so she could trap them," whispered the second child.

"Oh, my goodness, glory be," gulped the first child shuddering in his seat. "No wonder people stay away!"

Hansel and Gretel had heard enough. Hansel stopped shooting spitballs and Gretel stopped turning her best friend's hair inky blue. They looked at each other with gleaming eyes. And, because they were twins, they immediately knew what the other was thinking. They had to go there, to the witch's house, right away. This very second. No time to waste. Of course, this meant getting out of dreary, useless school... a small problem, but nothing to stop the twins, who were very used to tricking their way out of situations they didn't like.

Gretel quickly pretended to faint, falling off her chair with a loud groan and an even louder thunk.

Hansel immediately jumped out of his own seat and rushed to his sister's aid. "Don't worry, teacher," he shouted (because people always shout in emergency situations). "I'll take care of her! I'll see that she gets home where she can die in peace!"

With much huffing and puffing, Hansel slung the fakely fainted Gretel over his shoulder and carried her out of the little stone schoolhouse. As soon as they were outside, he dropped her on the ground.

"You need to lose weight," he wheezed, gasping for breath.

"That's nice coming from you, fatso," she snapped back.

They glared at each other and punched each other in the head for a minute or two, and then, suddenly remembering the gingerbread house, Gretel leapt to her feet.

"Let's go!" she roared (because people always roar when they're anxious to get on their way). "There isn't a moment to lose!"

"Yes, let's!" roared Hansel, who was also anxious to get going. "Let's find that house and eat every last bit of it!"

They ran as fast as their chubby little legs could carry them towards the forest, much to the surprise of their classmates, who were, of course, staring out the window in the manner that students always do while stuck in school.

"Gretel seems to have recovered, teacher," piped up one student, but the teacher was asleep and paid no attention.

Hansel and Gretel charged into the forest and headed straight for the gingerbread house. In mere moments, they had found it because, fortunately for them and unfortunately for Nana Myrtle and Peter, the gluttonous twins were very sensitive to the smell of candies, cookies, and cakes. They could sniff them out from miles away.

They crept up to the house very carefully.

"Do you think that wicked witch is around here somewhere?" whispered Gretel nervously.

"I think I can hear her licking her lips," stammered Hansel, straining his ears.

"I can hear her drooling," trembled Gretel, starting to sweat with fear.

"Let's flush her out," whispered Hansel, "so she can't sneak up on us when we're least expecting an attack."

Gretel nodded her head anxiously. She prayed that the witch would like the looks of her plump brother and would decide to eat him instead of her.

In the meantime, Hansel was hoping that the witch would think that Gretel was the tastier of the two and would choose her for her evening meal and leave him well alone.

With these pleasant, loving thoughts in mind, they started calling out, "Here witchee, witchee, here witchee, here girl." After they had repeated this a few thousand times and no witches came leaping out of the bushes, Gretel said, "I don't think she's here."

"She must have gone for a little hike through the woods," Hansel agreed.

"Or perhaps she's off gulping down children in some other spot," suggested Gretel happily.

Which of course she was ... hiking in the woods, that is, not gulping down poor wee tikes. Because, as you know, this was the day she had taken Peter hunting for duck eggs.

Comfortably confident that they weren't about to be eaten in the next few minutes and feeling tremendously hungry after all of their witch calling, Hansel and Gretel opened their greedy mouths wide, wider, and wider still. They began taking enormous bites out of everything they could lay their teeth on. They ate and ate and ate and ate and ate and ate and ate and ate....

"Try the roof," mumbled Hansel with his mouth full. "It's made out of red licorice."

"Try the walls," gulped Gretel, swallowing a piece of gingerbread. "They're too delicious to be believed."

"Try the dining room table. It's milk chocolate."

"Try this chair. It's a marshmallow."

"Try the bed."

"Try the lamp."

Before long, they had eaten everything: the roof, the walls, and all of the furniture. The only thing left where once the gingerbread cottage had stood was the big cast iron oven that Nana Mrytle used for all of her baking.

"Urp! I'm full," murmured Gretel contentedly, her stomach twenty times the size that it had been when she had woken up that morning.

"Me too!" belched Hansel, who looked as if his clothes were about to burst.

"I think I'll just have a little nap," sighed Gretel.

"The same goes for...," grunted Hansel, and he began to snore.

It was growing dark out when Nana Myrtle and Peter returned home with two baskets full of eggs. They were both looking forward to a nice dinner of pumpkin pie and chocolate brownies, which Nana Myrtle had baked just that morning before they set out.

"Hurrah for pumpkin pie! Hurrah for chocolate brownies!" Peter cheered. "Hurrah for...," suddenly, he stopped in his tracks. His eyes bulged out of his head and his mouth dropped open. "Oh, my goodness, gracious me, heavens above!" he shrieked. "Our house is gone! Our house is gone ... and the pie and brownies with it!"

Nana Myrtle, who had been smiling affectionately at Peter while he shrieked, snapped her head up so quickly that it almost flew off her neck. Her frail, old heart seemed to stop beating because there before her, where her lovely gingerbread house had been just that morning, was nothing but a cast iron oven and what looked to be two sleeping pigs dressed in silk, satin, and jewels, grunting, snuffling, and snorting as you would expect pigs to do.

"Oh no!" she wailed. "Oh mercy me! What terrible catastrophe has befallen us, my child!" She wailed on and on until, finally, the sound of her wailing woke the snoring Hansel and Gretel.

Hansel moaned, "What is that horrible racket?"

"I don't know," groaned Gretel. "But I wish it would stop. I have a stomachache."

When Nana Myrtle heard Hansel and Gretel talking, she knew that the two pigs lying in the ruins of her house were not pigs at all but were, in fact, children. (She had never met the Three Little Pigs so you can't really blame her for not knowing that pigs could also talk in the good old days.)

Hoping that the two grumpy children might be able to explain the mysterious disappearance of her home, Nana Myrtle ran in a hobbling way up to them and asked anxiously, "What happened here? Do you know, dear children? Please tell me if you do."

"AAAAAARRRRRRGGGGGGGGGHHHHHH! It's the awful, hideous, evil witch!" screamed Hansel. "Save me Gretel!"

"Save yourself," shrieked Gretel. "I don't want to be dinner!"

Hansel quickly pointed at his sister and whined, "She's tastier than I am! Eat her, dear, kind, loving witch!"

"He's fatter!" cut in Gretel.

"Am not!" yelled Hansel.

"Are too!" shouted Gretel.

"Am not!'

"Are too!"

"Am...."

"Children, children," interrupted Nana Myrtle, whose head was starting to hurt. "Nobody is going to eat anyone. I just want to know what happened to my charming little two-bedroom cottage? Do you know?"

"Why, we ate it of course," shot back Hansel rudely, who was feeling very brave now that he knew he wasn't going to be eaten.

"Some bits were burnt," said Gretel. "You should take more care. No wonder I have a stomachache."

"You ate it?" stammered Nana Myrtle. "But, but, that was Peter's and my house."

"Well, it was a stupid house," said Gretel.

"But it was the only one we had. Now we have nowhere to sleep," said the grandmother, fighting back worried tears.

"Sleep in the oven. It's big enough," said Hansel. Then he added, "See ya'! We've got to go. We must get home for dinner."

Just at that moment, almost as if Nana Myrtle really was a witch and had cast a spell, there was a great clap of thunder, and rain and hailstones and snow started pelting the earth and everyone on it.

"Oh, glory be!" shouted Gretel. "We'll be pummeled to death! Let's get in the oven so we can stay safe and dry, Hansel!"

"But, that's Peter's and my only shelter now," exclaimed Nana Myrtle, wringing her hands anxiously. "You have a home to go to…. We have no other place to stay warm and unpelted."

"Too bad for you," sneered Hansel.

"Yeah. Go crawl into a hole somewhere if you want to be warm. That's where worms like you belong anyway," added Gretel.

And with that, Hansel and Gretel climbed into the oven.

Desperate to protect her little grandson from the terrible storm, Nana Myrtle took Peter's hand and led him as quickly as her rickety legs would carry her into the deepest, deepest, *absolutely deepest* depths of the forest. She knew that there was a cave there that would provide some shelter for them.

Meanwhile, back in the oven, Hansel and Gretel were staying very dry, but not very warm.

"I'm freezing," complained Gretel. "Put some wood in the oven's firebox to warm us up, Hansel."

"Do it yourself," said Hansel through chattering teeth. "I'm not your servant."

"Please. Pretty, pretty, please," whined Gretel.

"Oh, all right, you spoilt little brat," grumbled Hansel. "How I ever got a sister like you, I can't imagine. You're not a thing like me." He opened the oven door and climbed out. There, stacked neatly under the oven, was a pile of wood and a book of matches, nice and dry and sheltered from the storm.

He tossed the wood into the firebox that was attached to the underbelly of the oven and set it alight with one of the matches.

"That's better," he said smugly. "Perfect."

He climbed back into the oven and said to his sister, "Satisfied now? It's lovely and warm in here. I hope that shuts you up once and for all."

Well, of course it did. In fact, it shut both of them up forever.

Which, really, was a very good thing.

Oh, and by the way, in case you were wondering, once the storm was over and they returned to the oven, Nana Myrtle and Peter found it empty of children but full of diamonds, emeralds, rubies, and other precious gems. These jewels made them so marvelously rich that they were able to buy a lovely stone mansion in the village, and they had plenty of gems left over to buy everything their hearts could ever desire.

And, so, they lived happily ever after.

"Hurrah!"

The End

When greed makes you from others take,
don't be surprised if you wind up baked.

Backword

And so, dear reader, we come to the end of Felicitatus Miserius's frightful book.

Remember to heed the lessons that fill its miserable pages or you too may end up with slugs living in your hair … if you live at all.

"Lessons?" you may well be asking. "What lessons? I know of none."

Well, my friend, if you saw no lessons within these terrible tales, close your eyes for a moment and reflect upon the behavior of Cinderella, Rapunzel, Red Riding Hood, Hansel and Gretel, and the Three Little Pigs… and then, I beg of you, do your best NOT to behave in that abominable fashion. If you DO choose to act like one or—good gracious me!—all of those horrible creatures, I am afraid that there may be no saving you. Your fault, not mine.

And, should the terrifying little Miserius creature show up at your door one day, as she almost certainly will if she hasn't already, please pass along to her my humblest respects. Then, tell her, if you would, that I've moved and am nowhere to be found.

Until next time, because there always is a next time,
Your friend,
Sir Jasper Gowlings

Acknowledgements

The creation of this book wouldn't have been possible without the love, support and inspiration provided by the following individuals:

My wonderful husband, John, who is living proof that there really are princes out there and dreams really do come true. Thank you for helping me to believe in myself and for making my life so perfect. I love you with all of my heart!

My amazing parents, who have filled my life with love and joy since the day I was born. Thank you for always being there for me. I love you more than words can say!

Margaret, whose generous spirit and loving heart brought comfort to everyone fortunate enough to know her. I miss you every day and will love you always.

Alison, Susan, John, Shawna and Kristen, who have forever been a source of tremendous inspiration, happiness and hope for me. I feel so blessed to be related to you and love you all very much.

Caroline, Jessica, James, Patrick, William, David, Evan, Fiona, JD and Ollie who have given me the chance to remain a child at heart. I hope that you grow up knowing just how wonderful you are and that all of your dreams come true. I love you!

Shirley Chiang, whose wonderful illustrations brought the stories in this book to life. You are truly the best, Shirley! Thank you from the bottom of my heart.

All of the amazing people at iUniverse, especially (in alphabetical order) Lauren Allen, Natalie Chenoweth, Jessica Flores, Steve Furr, Teresa Hale, Krista Hill, Ryan Hopkinson, Jessica Lynn McIntosh, Dayne Newquist, Liesl Schapker and Amy Tevault, without whom this book would never have gone anywhere. Thank you for believing in me and for all of your incredible advice and support. I will be forever grateful to you for making this book a reality. You are phenomenal!